TRAINS TO NOWHERE

And Other Stories of World War II

By

R. David Fulcher

ISBN: 0-75962-359-7

This book is printed on acid free paper.

1stBooks - rev. 07/03/01

TABLE OF CONTENTS

Page

1. WAKE UP CALL

Chris Burton's head hurt.

The screeching electric wail of the alarm clock seemed to come from everywhere, both inside his head and out.

What had it been last night? Poker? Monday Night Football? Had last night been a Monday at all?

It slowly filtered back to his mind's eye in disjointed images. George's basement. An old film, some black and white job. Bogart, maybe? *The Maltese Falcon*?

One thing about the night before was clear. Chris had drunk way too much. Ninety-nine bottles of Heineken on the wall were now somewhere near eighty.

He rolled over and poked a finger into the blinds. Sunshine darted into the room and Chris looked away. The clock on the nightstand read 9:30 AM. Next to the clock, in a non-descript frame, was a photograph of Sara and Bobby.

<u>What would they think now?</u> Here was husband and father, hung over and dead to the world at 9:30 on a weekday morning, in a stained T-shirt and boxer shorts while the rest of the world's dads were up and out working, cleanly shaven Ward Cleavers sprinting up the corporate ladder.

It was the same old shit, different day. Only today there was something behind the cotton dry mouth and bass drum blood pounding at his temples. Something had him really on edge, had put a screaming guitar lick behind his empty blues.

Whatever it was, it didn't change one thing. As sunlight spilled over the picture on the nightstand, it seemed to fix and catch hold on Sara's face, and like every other day Chris knew he was a failure.

* * * * *

"Chris, I'm not saying you have a problem with your drinking. I'm saying that you have a problem with your attitude. I know it's a hard time for you right now. Hell, when Cheryl divorced me it was all I could do to get out of bed. But you've got to be a man about this. Shit, Chris, the divorce is not even legal yet. You still have a chance to get her back."

"You're right, Phil. I know it," Chris said, rubbing a hand over the rough stubble of his chin.

"Listen. I've heard the boys upstairs. They have big plans for you, Chris. But they're starting to reconsider, you know, corporate stability and all that crap. Everyday that you come in looking like hell on the worse side of a drunk, and a hour and a half late, you shake their confidence. Don't ruin what you've built here, Chris. You've worked too hard. If you think you have an uphill battle to get Sara back now, just wait until you can't come up with the child support. That's the point of no return, buddy."

Chris sank his face into his hands and nodded.

"C'mon, Chris. Finish off that swill they call coffee so we can get to the staff meeting on time."

"Staff meeting? Is it Wednesday already? Oh shit!"

Chris gulped down the last cold, muddy gulp of coffee. It ran down his throat like mucus, and his stomach knotted and convulsed.

He got up and took his nausea into the conference room. They all seemed so perfect sitting there, so neat in their olive and charcoal suits holding their leatherbound portfolios.

All eyes fell on Chris as he entered the room. Finally somebody said it.

"Christ, Burton, you look like death warmed over!" The suppressed laughter of a busy workday, enhanced by the stress of traffic jams and stuffed inboxes, spilled into the room.

Chris hated Jack for saying it. He hated the way Jack's belly shook with the laughter and the way the florescent lights overhead made his bald head shine. Somewhere inside he hated being the butt of the joke, as opposed to safely nestled within the group.

"Jack, you old fat sack of shit. I would tell you about last night. I really would. But I promised her I would never breathe a word. Your wife, I mean."

The room exploded at this. Jack turned beet red. "Sonofabitch, sonofabitch," he kept muttering under his breath.

Mr. Parks entered the room, and suddenly their was silence.

"Well," he said, rubbing his large, ring-laden hands together, "I do hate to miss a good party. I must have the wrong room. I'm here to conduct business!" With this he slammed his fist against the polished oak table. The staff sat bolt upright in their seats like frightened rabbits.

As Mr. Parks strode across the room towards the head of the table each person issued a bright, artificial greeting as he passed.

"Good morning," Chris said meekly. Mr. Parks passed in front of him.

"Good morning, Mr. Burton, good morning indeed. I certainly like a chap who can keep all of the figures in his head! Look around you, Mr. Burton. Go ahead, don't be shy. So many tablets and charts! But no, not you! Mind like a steel trap."

Mr. Parks took a step forward, breathing down Chris' neck. "We shall see," he said sharply, and walked to his chair. His assistant smiled politely and followed behind him, carrying a steaming cup of coffee.

The meeting progressed as usual. Dollar amounts and status reports rolled off of their well-practiced tongues like twentieth-century mantras to capitalism.

There was something Chris couldn't get out of his mind, something shining brightly on the lapel of Mr. Park's perfectly pressed suit. Chris studied it from across the table. The lapel pin was fashioned into a small American flag.

Suddenly there was a blinding flash of light and a sharp pain at Chris' temples...

The day was sunny and bright. He ran through the woods. Behind him lay rolling green fields, scarred by a dark walled structure in the distance. His gray uniform dripped with sweat and his legs hummed with warm exhaustion. He heard birds singing overhead and felt the cold metal of a gun against his palm.

The wreckage of a small plane littered the forest floor ahead. The pilot was sitting Indian style on the ground. His face was burned and scratched, and he was trying to slow the steady flow of blood from his nose with one hand. The other hand was raised in surrender.

There was an American flag on the breast pocket of the pilot's flight suit.

Chris leveled the gun...

"Chris?"

"Huh?"

Chris opened his eyes. Mr. Parks had raised himself out of his chair and now stood with both hands gripping the edge of the conference room table. He was livid. "I was asking you about the Watts account?"

"Oh yes, uh... of course. I've been in close communication with Mr. Watts since he came on board with us two months ago. He continues to make large dividends on his extensive investments in mutual funds."

"And which foreign markets did you suggest to Mr. Watts for investment?"

"I'm not sure I follow," Chris replied. Someone coughed in the room and quickly stifled it.

"Surely you remember that Mr. Watts had a casual interest in foreign investment and that you were to prepare a report of the pros and cons of the various alternatives?"

"No sir, I don't. But I'll get on it right away." Someone was nervously tapping a pencil on the table, a metronome that seemed to divide the moment out in painful intervals.

"No, Chris, that won't be necessary. I've decided to hand over the Watts account to Jack."

Jack smiled across the table at Chris like a Cheshire cat.

"But—"

"I'm sorry, Chris. It's been mismanaged." Mr. Parks took a final sweep across the room. "Does anyone else have any other issues before we adjourn?"

Phil winked at Chris, then raised his hand. Chris silently mouthed "No!" to him but it was too late to intervene.

"Yes, Phil?"

"You may not be aware of this, sir, but Chris is going through a separation right now. It's a rough time for him. Don't let a small oversight destroy the excellent client relationship Chris has developed with Mr. Watts."

"I'm aware of Chris' situation, Phil. If I were you I would be more concerned with your own clients. Don't try to reverse my decision. It smacks of disloyalty and I simply will not tolerate it."

Phil nodded and shut his mouth. His wide, usually cheerful face looked sullen.

"Okay, then. Back to work everyone." Mr. Parks strode out of the room, his personal assistant close at his heels. One by one the staff members filtered out of the room.

After several minutes only Chris and Phil remained.

"Phil, don't stick your head out for me anymore. I'm just going to let you down."

"Forget about it, Chris. Why don't you go home? You look like crap and you must feel even worse. Call it a day. It will seem better after some aspirin and sleep."

"No, that's just what these piranhas would expect from me. I'm going to tough it out."

"Okay, you're the boss," said Phil, regaining his cheerful countenance. He slapped Chris on the back and left the room.

All the morning's tension and anxiety rose together as a ball of bile in Chris' throat.

Chris would tough it out. But first he was going to heave his guts out in the executive bathroom.

* * * * *

There was a buzzing in Chris' ear. It was annoying like the buzzing of his alarm clock, which had started this whole godforsaken day off to begin with, and he groped madly on his desk to shut it up. Finally his hand reached the intercom.

"Mr. Burton, are you in? Your wife is on the line."

Chris raised his head off of his desk. Jungle drums started to beat through the fuzzy haze of his head.

"Mr. Burton?" the secretary asked again.

"Yeah, I'm here...I mean, send it through please, Shannon."

"Right away, sir."

Chris picked up the receiver and placed his head back down on the blotter.

"Chris?" Sara's voice sounded much too loud, as if amplified through a megaphone.

"Hello, Sara."

"You sound terrible, Chris. Are you all right? Gail told me you and George went on a drinking binge last night."

"Yeah," Chris answered. <u>Tell Gail to mind her own friggin' business</u>, Chris wanted to say. If he was a miserable drunk, he was an even worse day-after drunk.

"Listen, I'm calling because I need a favor. I'm caught up in this huge project at work, and Cody's Little League game is tomorrow. Do you think you could make it in my place? It would mean a lot to him."

"I don't know, Sara. Things aren't going too well over here."

"I see," Sara replied coldly. "So you have enough time to drink with George, but you can't make your son's Little League game. Nothing's changed, Chris, nothing at all."

"Sara, I just lost a big account here. I'm still in shock. I just don't know what the situation will be here tomorrow."

"You've already lost me, Chris. Do you want to lose your son as well?"

"Of course not."

"Then get yourself together. You're going to shit."

There was a click and a dial tone. Chris didn't know what surprised him more, Sara's hanging up on him or saying the word shit.

The phone call upset Chris more than he wanted to admit. It filled him with guilt and nervous energy. "Shannon?" he asked through the intercom.

"Yes, Mr. Burton?"

"I'll be gone for the rest of the afternoon. Take any messages, please."

"Sure. Are you okay, Mr. Burton?"

"Just dizzy."

"I understand, Mr. Burton."

"You're a real dear, Shannon. Leave at four if you'd like. "

"Thank you, Mr. Burton, but somebody has to cover for you. Hope you feel better."

"I'll try," Chris replied meekly, knowing he wouldn't.

2. AWARENESS AND THE OPRAH SHOW

The ice cubes on his forehead were the only thing that held Chris to sanity. Everything around him was falling apart, and to make matters worse, he was experiencing these...what the hell would you call them? Visions? Daydreams? Nightmares?

But at least the ice cubes were perfect. Their coolness and simple geometric shapes calmed him as if he were lying next to the ocean. It was nice to slip into that mode, that escape where all problems could be left behind on a Caribbean wind.

The *Oprah Winfrey Show* on the television bothered him, made him remember that he was not lying under some tropical island sun but on the ragged couch in his beat up apartment in Arlington, Virginia.

<u>Where is the goddamn remote?</u> he asked himself. He rose, trying to keep the ice cubes on his forehead with one hand, and rummaged through the newspapers and magazines on the coffee table.

He tried in vain to shut out the talk show's dialogue. What was it this week? Transsexual midgets? Couples who wore monkey suits in the bedroom?

"We're back with my guest, Bruce Pearson. Today's topic is previous lives. Bruce, you say that you actually have visions of your previous life?" asked Oprah, crossing her arms and casually holding the microphone. She looked at the camera as if to say *I know, all-knowing audience, I don't buy it either.*

"Yes, quite often," the man answered calmly.

"What's it like? I mean, how does it start? Are you just driving down the road and suddenly you're seeing something else?"

"It's similar to that. First I feel a slight pain at my temple, like the beginning of a tension headache. Then there's a bright flash of light, almost blinding—"

Chris sat bolt upright, spilling the ice cubes onto the carpet.

There was some nervous laughter from the audience. "Don't mind them, Bruce. Boy, you all are ru-u-de! Continue. What do you see?" urged Oprah.

"Usually my visions are violent. I was a Roman centurion in my previous life, so most of my visions are of combat and war. I try to look away, but it's like a movie inside my head. Except that I can't switch it off. Closing my eyes doesn't help. I must have been exceptionally strong in my previous life. I mean, in my visions, I just keep hacking and hacking away with my sword, and the bodies just fall away. I'm never even sure just how many people I've killed in a battle. It's terrible, all the blood and the screams. I wish I could shut those visions out. I prefer the quiet ones, riding along in a chariot, viewing the Roman cities and countryside."

Chris freed the remote from under the corner of *People Magazine*. He clicked the television off. The nausea and pounding headache had gotten worse since he had sat up. The quietness of the previous moment had been destroyed along with the ice cubes, and Chris shook with fear as he rushed headlong towards the bathroom.

3. FLASHBACK

The small group huddled close to the fire. Flames and explosions highlighted the skyline of the Russian city of Kiev, splashing the sky orange and red for a moment, then back to total darkness. Then again: a flash of vivid color, then emptiness. It continued this way: flash, dark, flash, dark.

"Do you think we'll win?" One of the men by the campfire asked in German, a language that suddenly seemed as familiar to Chris as breathing. He studied the scene from above like a disembodied spirit.

"Haven't we always?" asked another.

"Yes, so far."

Their conversation was interrupted by the whistling descent of a nearby shell. The men paused, then turned back to their rations.

They were scared. They jumped inside every time they heard that sound. Often those volleys of death had been directed at them. Finally the sound faded in the distance and they could speak again.

"Did you see the black staff car that passed by us today?"

"Yes. It was SS."

"I don't understand why we need them," a young soldier with blonde hair stated emphatically.

"To control our prisoners," one replied.

"You mean to *kill* our prisoners."

Fire illuminated the city as a stack of bombs walked up the streets.

"A waste." The blonde one again this time.

"How so?" challenged another.

"It makes no sense. We have so many needs—uniforms, helmets, guns, boots—why do we kill our work force? Instead of using them to make bullets for our armies, we use our army's bullets on them. And there is no honor in such killing for a soldier. It is a disgrace."

"Hans, you do not understand. This is not like the Great War. There are no rules of engagement, no code of honor. Bombs are now dropped on city streets, not command posts. It is kill or be killed, nothing else but this. The Fuhrer has a plan. We and the SS are the executors of his plan. We cannot expect to understand all of his reasons. His mind is an emperor's mind. Would anyone question a Caesar? An Alexander the Great? A Bismarck? If not, then do not question the Fuhrer."

"Haven't you heard the stories?" the blonde one contested. "The old, the infirm, even the children are slaughtered. They are gassed and their bodies are burned."

"It is no different than from what any other country does to its prisoners of war."

"It is wrong. It is *evil*."

"Careful, Hans. It may be conversation to us, but such talk would be considered treason to the death head squads."

The blonde one sighed and looked down at the frozen earth. His warm breath steamed forth from his nostrils and mouth, and although no one heard it, the words *it is wrong* were formed in that cloud.

4. MYSTERIES REVEALED

Chris' palm sweated as he held the receiver in his hand. He could barely contain his excitement. Finally, after an endless series of rings, someone picked up on the other end.

"Hello, George?"

"Well, well, well. If it isn't Chris Burton, the town drunk, the local yokel boozehound. Chris, Chris, took a piss, drank too much, and the toilet he missed —"

"Cut the crap, George."

"Alright. How are you feeling?"

"Like hell."

"Well, for what it's worth, Gail gave me an earful for letting you get into that condition. "

"She's a good woman," Chris replied.

"Yes, she is. She's got this thing about defending lost causes, though."

"Real funny, George. No really, I'm cracking up."

"So what's up? Gail's bringing out the dessert soon, but if you need me, I'm listening. Did you speak with Sara lately?"

"Yes, earlier today. For once, that's not what I called about."

"Hmmm…now I am confused."

"I called to ask you something."

"Shoot," George replied.

There was a moment of silence over the line.

"What do you think about reincarnation? I mean, do you think it's possible?"

"Whoa! That's a pretty loaded question. Any more ringers you're hiding?"

"Maybe. I can't tell you yet."

"Chris, are you doing alright? I didn't mean to mention this, but Gail said she saw you come home early this afternoon. Did something happen at work?"

"Yeah, but that's not why I called. I lost the account."

"You mean 'The Account'? The account that would make you a partner of the firm?"

"Yes."

"Chris, why the hell didn't you tell me you had important work to do in the morning? I would have made sure to cut you off after one drink."

"It's not that. I've been letting this go to pot since Sara left. I really don't want to talk about it. Could you just answer my question?"

"Yeah, sure. Reincarnation...hmmm. Well, the Jewish faith tells me *not* to believe in it, but off the record, I think it's possible. Even I've felt deja vu."

"Really?"

"Yes, the first time I went to Israel. Right off the plane I began to feel like the place was familiar to me. It was really uncanny. I even knew my way around, which is completely mind-boggling, considering my poor sense of direction. I never told anyone about it, of course. What do you say? 'I know this place, but I have never been here before in my life.' People will think you are out of your gourd. It is really amazing, the supernatural is accepted in blind faith when it is described in a religious text, but other phenomena, such as clairvoyance, ghosts, and telekinesis are strictly taboo when discussed outside of religion. I've never really understood why it is that way, but it is."

"Well, what did you, George Kushner, think?"

"I think I have lived there before."

"Did you have any visions?"

"You mean did I actually see myself living in an earlier time? No. It was just a feeling, an intuition. But it was enough for me."

"Do you think you were a good person, George? Back then, I mean."

"I think I was the *same* person."

"Come again?" asked Chris.

"It's like this. To me, reincarnation is merely a transfer of spirit, the transport of soul between two physical bodies. The substance of the individual, those things that make that person what they are, remain the same. Their looks may change, their social status, maybe even their sex, but *they* stay the same. So in a previous life, or in the next life for that matter, I would still be the being you know as George and you would still be the being I know as Chris. Of course, I would come back even manlier and you would come back in a dress."

"Thanks."

"GEORGE! Would you put that thing down and come eat with your family!" Gail Kushner's voice shrilled in the background.

"Listen, I better run."

"Okay."

"Chris?"

"Yes?"

"When you have this thing worked out, I'd love to know what it's all about. You always have a friend here, okay?"

"Yeah, thanks George. That means a lot right now." Chris put the receiver down. His headache had long since passed, but now he had other things to think about.

5. SENBRUCH

The Senbruch Concentration Camp never sleeps. There are always trains coming and going, always the motion and sounds of loading and unloading, always guards passing, always spotlights sweeping, always dog barking, always smoke of human fat frying, frying in eternal ovens.

In rare quiet times, one can hear the wind wash through the barbed wire fences like a slow moan.

Inside the barracks there is always needing needing, hunger hunger, spit and blood and aching bones. The corrugated tin roofs shed no starlight but if one is a dreamer one can still see them shine in the night sky. Occasionally there is the distant rumble of bombers in the distance but even if one is a dreamer a bomb is too much to wish for.

Across the camp young lovers embrace. There is no time here for ceremony, no time for religion. God is outside of the camp, or dead. There is only time for a rushed embrace, hastened words, and the almost painful promise: "When this is all over, we shall marry and buy a home. We shall have many children and worship in God's temple."

Outside, dawn is approaching. The guards change shifts and the spotlights dim their fevered glances.

It is tomorrow at Senbruch, but it is also today, and the yesterday before. It is last night.

6. THE VISITOR FROM BEFORE

Chris Burton slept. Outside, beyond his bedroom window, the moon hung fat and heavy in the network of branches. The night was silent.

Chris Burton slept. But his body was awake. The small hairs on the nape of his neck stood on end and goosebumps peppered his exposed skin.

His *body* sensed the man standing next to the bed, but for the moment Chris Burton did not. Although it was mid-August in the city, the room was cold, and the body of Chris Burton began to shiver. He groped for the sheets he had carelessly flung aside, but his hands did not find them. He instinctively wrapped his arms around his chest and curled up into a fetal position, but the cold continued to invade his body—it ran cool in his veins and burned like snow in the marrow of his bones. Eventually it approached his heart with icy fingers, and this set off alarms in the consciousness called Chris Burton, and in an instant he was awake.

* * * * *

Chris awoke with a start. <u>Must have been a nightmare</u>, he told himself, dripping cold sweat and gasping for air. It read 2:32 A.M. on the clock on the nightstand, and the dim red glow of the stoplight outside on the street strobed through the window.

And there was someone in the room with him.

"Wh-Who?" Chris stammered.

The young man was tall and slender. His blue eyes were striking against his grey uniform, but extremely sad. He held a scroll in his left hand.

"What do you want?" Chris whispered, sliding up against the headboard of the bed. The man lifted his hand, presenting the scroll to him.

With the movement, the man's image jumped and flickered like a reel of old movie footage, and for an instant Chris could see *through* the man.

"My God," Chris whispered, and "My God" once again.

The man smiled faintly. The image flickered, jumped, flickered, jumped—then was gone.

Chris shook uncontrollably. He finally found the sheets and pulled them up to his neck. Shutting his eyes tightly, and taking deep breaths, he counted backwards from fifty.

Finally he opened them. The apparition was gone. But then something else terrified him all over again.

A scroll rested on the bed beside him.

7. GRANDFATHER

The boy stood on his toes to touch the sunflower which towered over him. He wondered what the black kernels within the yellow fringe of petals felt like.

His hand stopped several inches from the flower's face. There was no more body to stretch.

Suddenly he felt himself being lifted from the earth. He laughed with delight and caressed the dark seeds.

"What do you think, Hans?" His grandfather held him easily in the air.

"It feels...funny, I think. I thought it would be soft. Are you sure people eat them?" he asked.

"Yes," the man replied, laughing heartily and setting Hans back down on the ground.

High above the sun shone brilliantly. It seemed to Hans that summer was the season of green and orange.

They entered the house through the patio door. Strains of classical melodies were playing softly on the radio. In the corner, Hans' grandmother was painting a picture.

Hans bounded onto her lap.

"Oh, Hans, vorsicht! Do you like it?" she asked, pointing to the canvas.

The boy drank in the ruby hues of the painted fruit. "It makes me hungry," he replied.

The grandparents exchanged amused glances.

Suddenly the music on the radio was interrupted. "The Jews have taken our jobs. They have betrayed Germany by giving information to the Allies during the war, stabbing our sons in the back. Do not let them take the future of the German Reich!" The speaker's voice was replaced by a thirsty mob crying "Sieg Heil!"

The boy jumped up and down with the mantra: "Sieg Heil! Seig Heil!" he cried out with excitement.

Hans' grandfather knelt down in front of him. His face was grave.

"Hans, I never want you to do that again. Do you understand?"

"But—"

"Please, Hans. For me." The boy nodded.

"Give me your hand." The boy offered his grandfather his hand and was led to the couch.

"Hans, would you enjoy some Pommes Frites?" his grandmother asked.

The boy shook his head up and down quickly, a wide grin spreading across his face. The woman got up, ruffled his sunlit blonde hair, and left the room.

"Hans, do you know what 'Seig Heil' stands for?"

"Yes, Vater showed me. It means 'Hail Victory.' You put your arm out like this—"

"Don't," his grandfather urged, holding down his arm.

"Opa, I don't understand. Vati says that it is a cheer for Germany. He says it is for the men in the brown shirts. He says that the men will make Germany strong again, and that we shall defeat France!"

"Your father is wrong, Hans. The men in the brown shirts are not kind or good. They get pleasure from hurting people because they are different from us. That is wrong, Hans. Do you know the woman who taught your grandmother how to paint?"

"Yes, she always brought me sweets. I liked her very much."

"Yes, she is a fine woman. Do you know what the brown shirts would do to her?"

"No," Hans replied, a bit scared.

"They would destroy her home. They would take her away from her husband and children. They would beat her and put her in a cage like an animal."

"But why? She is so nice!"

"Because she worships God differently than we do."

"I don't understand," the boy replied, utterly frustrated.

The man spun Hans around on his lap so that he could look into the boy's eyes. It was hard for him to think of Hans, the beautiful boy with the blue, innocent eyes in the years ahead under Nazi tyranny. He had to protect him, from both his father and this new hateful Germany.

"Look at me, Hans. Listen to me as if I were dying."

The boy gasped but his grandfather put a finger on his lips. The boy's grandmother stopped in place as she was about to enter. The hearty smell of the fried potatoes wafted across the room.

"Nazi is a bad word, Hans. Make it so in your life. If the Nazis have their way, there will be no sunflowers. There will be no books, no paintings, no music. There *will* be fire. There *will* be guns and bombs. There *will* be people bleeding, many, many, many people bleeding and buildings burning. This is the Nazi's Germany. This is the Third Reich. If they win, all will be dead." He squeezed the boy's frail arm and stared firmly into his eyes.

"If they win, all will be dead."

There was a moment of stillness during which Hans could not look away from the graying man's burning eyes. He felt his heart racing in his chest.

"Do you understand?"

Hans nodded.

"You will remember what I said?"

Hans nodded.

"Do you promise not to tell your father about this?"

Hans nodded.

The man pulled the boy close to his chest and hugged him. "Thank you, Hans. I love you."

"I love you, Opa."

The grandmother made her way over to them.

"Here is your Mittagessen, Hans."

The boy giggled as he scooped up the fried snacks. He did not understand what had just transpired; he would not understand for years. But he would not forget the words:

If they win, all will be dead.

8. A CONVERSATION BEFORE DINNER

"George, what do you think about the Holocaust?"

"What's this? After one movie I'm suddenly no longer your buddy George, but I'm George the Jew? Suddenly I have a history, even a religion?" George's voice dripped with sarcasm.

Chris didn't know what the hell George was talking about but he recognized George's asshole voice right off the bat.

"What the hell are you talking about? What movie?"

"*Schindler's List*, what else?"

"*Schindler's List*? I thought we saw *The Maltese Falcon* with Bogey."

George's narrow body rocked with laughter. His face was bright red and he kept slapping his knee. "Oh ho! Ho oh! I figured as much. You said the same thing while you were drunk, but I thought you were joking. You really should avoid getting that shit-faced on a week night."

"Okay, okay. You don't have to be such a wisenheimer about it. I guess that's what's got me thinking about it, the Holocaust I mean. C'mon George, I really want to know what you think."

"You're serious, aren't you?" George asked.

Chris nodded.

George stood up and closed the door to his study. "I'd rather not let the kids hear this. It confused them enough in Hebrew school," he said softly, closing the door.

"Well, then...okay, okay," he muttered, returning to his seat, "Sorry, I'm not used to discussing this with—"

"A goy?" interjected Chris.

"Well, I would have put it more politely, but yes, a goy. It's a very sensitive topic for Jews, as you might understand."

"I understand," Chris replied. "Forget about it if it upsets you."

"No, no, I'm glad you want to talk about it. When you hear most people talk about the Holocaust—and when I say most people I mean most Jews—all you hear about are the camps. The camps were this and the camps were that. This happened at Dachau, this was the way it was at Auschwitz. But when I think about it, I think about the trains."

"Trains?"

"Yes, trains. You know, Chris, choo-choo's?"

"George, you're being a wise ass again."

"Alright, sorry. As I was saying, I think about the trains. These trains run all through the night. They are black and have snow-white skulls on the front of the engines. Blood-red Nazi flags are mounted on the engine, and the sides of the box cars are decorated with swastikas of the same color red. Limbs are sticking out between the boards of the freight cars—arms, legs, smooth with youth and calloused with age all mixed together. If you listen closely you can hear the cars breathing their great shuddering gasps of despair. They are ghost trains, you see, because the people inside of those freight cars are the living dead."

George paused and licked his lips. He seemed very far away.

"The trains ramble through the desolate land. The vibrations of the tracks as the trains roll overhead shake loose the few remaining panes of glass left in the windows of empty houses. They are houses now, not homes, because the things that made them a home—pictures of loved ones, family heirlooms, food, life—have all been destroyed. There are thousands of these houses across Germany, Poland, Czechoslovakia, Lithuania; all connected by the sense of absence that permeates the walls and floors. It is one huge kibbutz of sorrow."

Chris suddenly realized he was shaking. He had never seen his friend like this before. George's eyes had become small and intense, and his voice was slow and deep, as if it wasn't George at all but rather an alien presence using George's body as a mouthpiece. He was slumped forward in his easy chair in a tense, awkward position.

"In some of the houses belongings have been left behind, and as the black trains rumble past each picture frame, each knife and fork tell their own story of Nazi brutality and rape. It is a counter-melody, and it is weak against the lustful song of hate and power sung by the screeching wheels of the trains.

"The amazing thing about these trains, you understand, is that they really don't go anywhere, or more precisely they travel into nothingness. Thousands and thousands of people board these trains." George paused again for a moment, his eyes tearing.

"And they are never seen again. They break up families into columns, and force them to board different trains, quickly without goodbyes. But this is the last goodbye. They are never seen again. Their entire existence is reduced to a handful of ash which filters down from the sky."

George turned his palm upward, as if to catch something. He was silent for a long time as he cried.

"George?" Chris asked.

"George?" he repeated.

"Sorry. It just really makes one think about how good we Jews have it now."

"George, do you suppose there were any good Nazis?"

"Come again?"

"Do you think that any of the Nazis were decent, at any level?" pressed Chris.

"You probably shouldn't ask a Jew this question if you really want an objective answer."

"I know, but tell me anyway."

"Well, obviously the upper echelon of the Nazi party was corrupt at best, evil and homicidal at worst. I don't believe there was any good in those men. Perhaps some of the soldiers before they were fully indoctrinated into Nazi philosophy. After all, they were only young men, many of them boys, really."

Chris pressed further. "What about at the camps?"

"At the camps? I don't think so. The horrors of the concentration camps were conducted and supervised by butchers, I'm sure of that. After all, it was one of the SS's primary responsibilities."

"But isn't it true that every man of age was forced to join the military? What if you were forced into it?"

"I don't know, Chris. I just don't think it's possible. Why all these questions? Does this have something to do with our phone conversation the other evening?"

Chris ignored George and continued. "Do you think I'm a bad person, George?"

"No Chris, I don't. A little f'd up, maybe, if you'll excuse the expression, but—" George's eyes grew large. "My God, Chris! You think you *were* a Nazi in a previous life!" George blurted out.

"I'm not sure. I know it's crazy. But I keep having these visions. I've also got this," Chris handed George the scrolled parchment given to him by the ghostly visitor the night before. George could feel the age of the document on his fingers. He noticed the small Nazi seal in dark ink where it was taped shut.

"Where did you find this? In the pocket of your grandfather's raincoat?" George inquired.

"Don't ask."

There was a knock at the door to the study. "Boys, dinner time!" Gail's melodious voice called out.

"Okay, dear, we'll be right out," George sang back.

"C'mon, Chris. We'll talk more after dinner. We'll both feel better then."

"Agreed," Chris responded. They rose from their seats.

George placed the scroll on his desk. He took one troubled look back at it before he shut the door, and then he turned out the light.

* * * * *

"George, that really hit the spot. I'll say it once again, that Gail is quite a catch."

"Anything would seem good to you after all of those Hungry Man TV dinners, Chris."

Chris settled into the easy chair with his hands on his stomach. George took a seat at his desk. Spinning the globe on the desk, George spied the scroll. He had briefly forgotten about it during dinner.

Chris had his eyes closed as he reclined in the easy chair.

"Chris?" George asked.

"Yo," Chris responded, not opening his eyes.

"I have a friend at James Madison. He has a doctorate in German Studies. I believe he's out of town through the end of this week, but if I could deliver this to him for analysis when he gets back would you be interested?"

Chris opened his eyes and moved the recliner into an upright position. "Very much. I feel like I'm going crazy. These visions, or experiences, depending on your beliefs, have really messed with me. If someone is trying to communicate with me, particularly if it is a previous *me*, I feel like I really need to try to receive the message. There's only one thing that scares me, George."

"What's that?" he asked.

"What if it is really terrible? What if my soul is fundamentally evil? You must admit, the signs have not been encouraging."

"I consider myself a good judge of character, Chris. You're like a brother to me. If that were true, I would have picked up on it years ago."

"But how can you be sure?"

George shrugged. "Call it intuition. I'll drive this document out to James Madison Monday. Not only should my friend be able to translate it but he should also be able to shed some light on its place in the Nazi military subculture. That way we'll know if it's an order for more toilet paper at the front or a declaration of war."

"You mean *my* subculture," Chris said hollowly.

"Ah, Chris. I find your self-pity boorish and utterly unappealing," George said this in a mocking, rather poor English accent.

Chris cracked a smile. "Listen, dinner was great. I really appreciate the company."

"Anytime," George replied, getting up to walk Chris out.

George paused by the front door.

"Chris, there's something else I should tell you about the Holocaust, and those trains which give me nightmares."

"What's that?"

"A single menorah burned during the Holocaust. It shed ribbons of light across those dark tracks. It was the Menorah of Hope, and it symbolizes the strength of my people. It still burns today."

"That's very poetic, George. Beautiful, actually."

"Think about it," George said, slapping Chris on the back. "Goodnight."

"Goodnight," Chris returned, wishing he had his own light to fight back the clawing fears that hounded and jumped at him as he walked home.

9. NUREMBERG

Chris looked at himself in the mirror. His eyes were bloodshot and carried heavy black bags which contrasted with his pasty complexion. Dinner at George's and a shower had made him *feel* human again, but he still did not look the part. He sighed as he squeezed toothpaste onto his toothbrush. Even his teeth looked hairy.

There was a pressure at his temples, a dull tension which had become frighteningly familiar. Chris dropped his toothbrush. Flashes of pain shot to his temples, and he gripped the side of the sink. Then there was a flash of light like the sun exploding inside of his brain...

The young man had never been so proud. The citizens of the Reich covered the bleachers as if they were hung in mid-air, cheering and celebrating the new Germany—cheering and celebrating him.

Somewhere in the bleachers, up there with the jubilant masses, was his father. He could see him in his mind, his father's strong, broad face beaming with pride that only a son can bring a father. His father's words of the week before filtered back to him: "Respect the Fuhrer. He stands for the Germany I knew when I was a boy, before it was cut up and shamed by the Allies and the Jews. He will make Germany great again. Serve him with pride, Hans. Serve him well."

The young man drank in the summer breeze, wanting the moment to last forever. The hurdles and the track awaited him, but he was eager only for this, this overwhelming sense of pride and belonging. Every Nazi banner and standard was a testimony to this moment, to this Germany. Every eagle and swastika was a testimony to this people.

Their leader approaches the podium, the favor of a hundred thousand pairs of eyes.

"Sieg Heil!" he shouts in salute.

"Sieg Heil!" the crowd roars back, and Hans smiles and extends his arm with them.

10. THE BALLPARK

Like always, the parking on Wilson Boulevard was horrendous. Chris parked several blocks away and walked through the lazy mid-day streets of Arlington, Virginia. He was still coming down from his drinking binge two nights before, but the August sun felt good on his face, and the cool autumn-like breeze which swept across the street kept him from sweating in his suit.

Chris surveyed the townhomes and small Spanish groceries as he made his way to the field. He had walked these streets with Sara years before when they had started dating. Today, Chris couldn't even be sure they were the same people.

He imagined Cody at baseball practice, his dirty blonde hair and blue eyes contrasting with his loud Red Devils uniform, gritting his teeth as he cracked another ball deep into the outfield. He thought of the faces of the young men at the Nuremberg games he saw last night in the vision, and they looked like Cody's when he played ball.

Chris tried to push this thought away and stepped up his pace. He was soon in sight of the field, and he maneuvered around the fence. The coach was giving all of the small devils a pep talk, and at its conclusion they jumped up and down in time to the chant of "Go Devils!" Chris caught Cody's attention and the boy rushed over to the fence.

"Dad!" he yelled gleefully, grabbing onto the fence links.

"Hi, buddy," Chris replied, placing his hands over his son's.

"Aren't you supposed to be at work or something?" Cody asked.

"Even us old guys get lunch, Champ."

Cody looked down into the dirt, "You're not staying for the game, are you."

"I wish I could."

Cody nodded.

"Mom's pretty pissed at you," he said matter-of-factly.

"I know, son."

"Dad, when are you moving back home?"

"I don't know, Cody. I really don't." Chris sensed his son's disappointment.

"Do you still love mom?"

"Yes, very much."

"She loves you, too."

"Oh yeah?" Chris asked. "Says who?"

"I heard her talking to Ms. Kushner on the phone. She says she loves you but you're still a mess."

A whistle blew, and the opposing team, decked in blue, took the field. "Gotta go, Dad! Will you watch? Just for a little bit? We're really going to kick some butt!" Cody cried mischievously.

"Sure."

"Great! Love you, dad." Cody squeezed his father's hand briefly between the fence.

"I love you, too. Knock 'em dead." Cody winked and sprinted over to the Red Devil dugout.

And for a few slow minutes of Chris Burton's life, there was a strange sort of misplaced peace.

11. THE ELEVATOR HOUSE

The prisoners at Senbruch worked hard. If they did not, they were shot. It was simple: work hard, live and eat. Not much, but *something* to eat. Work hard, live to see the sun tomorrow, the next bowl of soup. Perhaps tomorrow a fall breeze will come through the fences and bring coolness. Perhaps tomorrow the machines will break and we will be sent back to the barracks. And the impossible dream: perhaps tomorrow this war will be over. Keep on. One day at a time. Have faith. Have blind faith because what your eyes see is the blood and the ribs poking through skin and the endless summer snow which is really not snow but something all together much worse.

The prisoners at Senbruch know their camp. They know each plot of earth and each strand of barbed wire. They know the barracks, the latrines, the light poles. They know the small brick building set apart from the rest that houses the elevators. They know it because their children had gone into that building and never had come out.

If there was a hell worse than Senbruch, they believed it was reached by those elevators. They knew Hans Richter as he strode across the camp to the elevators, and they believed he was one of that hell's keepers.

It was a humid day, and Hans sweated as he walked towards the elevator house. The prisoners did not look at him, they averted their eyes as they moved to and fro with shiny helmets, canteens, and ammunition belts. But despite this, they *saw* him.

He knew they were watching him. He could feel their gaze beneath his skin.

He kept walking. He did not want to look at them with their stick-like bones holding up their prison uniforms like surreal hangers. It was too late for them. They were unreachable. But for those below, the children, there was still hope.

Hans carried his illusion of contempt and authority until he was safely inside the elevator house. As the operator cranked the door closed, he sighed with relief and hung his head. It remained this way as the metal box clanked down through the earth to hell.

12. LIVING SINGLE

The pot was boiling over. Chris sprang out of the couch, slid on several sections of *The Washington Post* which were spread out on the floor, and careened into the kitchen. He quickly grabbed several pot holders from the counter and lifted the pot over to another burner. Inside a tangled mass of spaghetti swirled like an angry tempest. He turned the burner down and stirred the noodles as the water descended back down to a safe level. After a moment he returned the pot to the original burner. The familiar trumpet-like introduction of the six o'clock news sounded in the background.

Chris grabbed the remote and surfed the channels for something of interest. Beyond the windows it was still light outside, and as he watched the steady flow of traffic move through the city he felt useless and restless. He couldn't remember the last time he had actually gotten home on time. He felt like a retiree who finally got the time off he always wished for and now wanted to give it all back.

But he was under strict orders from his boss, and considering his precarious position at the firm lately, he went along with it. To some extent it was a great relief. He had never been on the sidelines before at work, he had always been a star. He watched Jack and the other account managers come and go from the office in a frenzied rush, watched them as they checked their watches, grabbed files, and made rushed phone calls before dashing out again to the client site while Chris and the other bench warmers performed routine follow up calls on long dead leads.

Lunch was the high point of the day now. He ate with Phil and got all of the good skinny on the firm's accounts. It was information he hoped he could use someday soon. In the meantime, he had to bide his time, pacing in the office like a caged tiger. Phil's offbeat humor improved Chris' mood somewhat, but only temporarily it seemed. By two o'clock he was back in the dumps again, counting the paper clips in his drawer for the thousandth time and rolling pencils across his desk.

He tried to turn his anger towards his boss, Mr. Parks, and several times was on the verge of storming into his office and calling him the biggest, dickless, baldest sack of crap he ever knew or worked for. In his saner moments, he knew Mr. Parks was doing exactly what any good manager would do. If an employee's personal life interferes with work to the point to where the accounts suffer, then adjustments must be made. He was lucky to be working at all.

Chris stopped surfing through the channels when he reached the *Roseanne* show. The show's introduction, which showed the family eating Chinese food together, touched something inside of him. Sure, he was no John Goodman, and Sara was a long cry from Roseanne, but family *is* family, no matter what the shape, size, or color.

There was a percolating sound from the kitchen, and Chris suddenly remembered the spaghetti sauce. He dived over the couch and scrambled into the kitchen. In his rush he forgot about the hotpads, and the lid of the saucepan burned his hand and went flying downwards.

It crashed onto the floor like a cymbal, and spikes of pain caused Chris to double-over and grab his head...

Chris could see through alien eyes. He was in another's body, a soldier's body by the look of the uniform.

His own body, the vacated shell which was rubbing its temples to put out the pain and blinding light, remained suspended in 1996. A pilot was crouched down in front of him, level with the barrel of his Mauser rifle.

"Give me your gun," the soldier commanded the American pilot.

The pilot fumbled with his holster, his hand slicked with blood. He fished out his government issue .45 and handed it to Chris grip-first.

Suddenly, dogs could be heard in the distance. The smell of the burning wreckage of the P-51 Mustang fighter plane filled Chris' head, and the pilot's pistol felt cool and heavy in his palm.

"Quickly," the soldier demanded, pulling the man up by the collar. "Over here, behind the tree. Make sure you don't make a sound."

"Name: John Bower, rank: Second Lieutenant, serial number—"

"Silence!" the soldier hissed. He placed the pistol against the pilot's head and cocked back the hammer. Now footsteps could be heard in the nearby woods. Suddenly a German soldier burst into the clearing, his Walther P-38 drawn at the ready.

The soldier that was Chris Burton pushed the gun more firmly against the pilot's head. "Say nothing," he hissed, this time in broken English.

The soldier advanced across the clearing cautiously, like a patient hunter.

A step forward. A glance to the right.

Stop. Listen. Advance, now, slowly, slowly...

There was a single report that ripped through the forest.

The soldier in the clearing dropped dead.

The American pilot looked on, stunned and beside himself, while his captor dropped the pistol next to the dead German.

The dogs could be heard again, this time more clearly.

"Quickly! The dogs are close!"

The soldier draped his arm around the pilot and the two dashed through the woods, tripping in the thorny undergrowth.

They finally came to rest at the edge of a streambed.

"Why are we stopping?" the pilot asked.

The soldier ignored him, and instead began to frantically dig away at the dirt on the bank of the stream.

"Help me, if you can. There is a small door here."

The American crouched down and together they dug with their hands, blackening their fingernails in the rich soil. Soon, one edge of a buried door became visible, and then the entire door.

Together, they pulled on the iron ring at the door's center. They braced their legs in the dirt but the door would not budge.

"We must, we must!" uttered the soldier in ragged breaths. "Once again, on three. Put your shoulder into it, but watch your injury."

The men and dogs were very close now.

"One—" they tightened their grip on the ring.

"Two—" they dug in their boots.

"Three!" Throwing their combined weight into it, the door sprang open with a pop! and the two men went sprawling. The soldier helped the pilot to his feet.

"Take this," he instructed the pilot, placing a scroll with a Nazi seal embossed on it into the other man's hand.

"I don't understand. I should be in Stalag Luft by now," the pilot stated, plainly amazed.

"We haven't much time, get in."

The man stepped into the small door and entered the low stone corridor. "Hey, there's electricity in here!" he exclaimed, his voice muffled by the streambed above him.

"Yes! Continue traveling towards the light. Further along you should find an alcove with fresh bread, water, and bandages. After several hours of travel the tunnel will end. At this point, knock three times on the ceiling of the corridor. It is the floor of an abandoned farmhouse. Friends will be there waiting for you. They will smuggle you into France and then into England from there."

"But—" the soldier pleaded.

The soldier held up his hand in negation. "We have no time. Deliver the document I have entrusted to you to British Intelligence. Tell them your story."

"Mach schnell!" a voice cried to the left. Confirmations of this command seemed to come from all sides of the forest, accompanied by the staccato barks of the dogs.

"You must leave now," the soldier commanded. He placed his hand on the edge of the door and began to close it.

"Wait!" the pilot cried out.

"Was?" the soldier asked in German, visibly tense.

"Thank you," the American said, grabbing the soldier's arm. "Danke."

The soldier nodded quietly and slammed the door shut.

Underground, the pilot could hear the soldier above working the mud frantically to cover the false entrance.

The pilot crawled forward on his hands and knees. The passageway was damp and cramped. In the distance, several hundred yards in front of him, a dim light shone like a star. Despite the burning wound and his precarious position behind enemy lines, the pilot smiled to himself.

For where there is light, there is hope.

13. ANGELIC REPOSE

Chris woke up and saw an angel.

Sara smiled sweetly down at him. "Are you finally awake, sleepy head?"

Thinking he was dreaming, Chris murmured aloud a half-whispered, "Sara?" As his eyes focused and the image of her remained, he attempted to get out of bed.

Sara placed her hand on his chest. "Don't get out of bed. You're very sick." Chris settled back into the bed, and Sara began wiping his forehead with a damp washcloth. It bothered Chris, this unfamiliar intimacy.

"What are you doing here?" he asked.

"George told me you had a fever. He also told me that you were having...well, other problems, I guess."

"What did he tell you?" Chris was now fully awake.

Sara deferred the question momentarily, instead dipping the washcloth into a bowl on the nightstand and squeezing out the excess water. Droplets of sweat rested on her brow and concern clouded her soft blue eyes. "He said that you were having headaches and visions. He said that you believe you were a Nazi in a previous life." She averted his eyes, and toyed with the washcloth as she told him this.

"You don't believe it, do you?" Chris asked.

"Chris, I'm worried about you. I know how upset you are over the separation." She washed his face quickly, nervously now.

"What about the scroll? Did he mention the scroll?"

"Yes. Yes, he did."

"WELL?" Chris asked impatiently.

"Well what, Chris? What am I supposed to say about all of this? I know you're under a lot of pressure. I'm just here to help."

"Sara!" he exclaimed, sitting up once again.

"Chris, please lay back down."

"No, goddamn it, I won't! We may be separated, but I'm still the man you married. I'm still the father of your child. I deserve your trust at a minimum."

"It's very hard for me, Chris. You are the man I married and the father of my child. That's why I know that you couldn't be right about this. You're a good man. There must be some other logical explanation, something we can't yet understand. I don't know anything about the afterlife, or reincarnation, or any other mystical crap. I do know you, and there's not an ounce of hatred in you, for Jews or anybody else...except, no, forget it."

"Sara! Finish what you were saying. I don't have hatred for anybody except who?"

Sara looked at him, then looked down at the washcloth clutched in her hand. "Except maybe for me," she said softly and began to cry.

"Oh, Sara. Honey, no."

"I'm sorry, Chris. It feels that way sometimes. I couldn't tell you before, but now, now things are different. I really have to go, Chris. I'm glad you're feeling better."

She gathered her purse up off the chair and began walking towards the door.

"Sara, please wait!" Chris pleaded.

She paused by the door.

"Did Cody tell you that I stopped by his Little League game?"

"Yes, he also told me you were too busy to stick around for it. Same old story, I guess. All work and no play makes Chris a dull boy." She removed a kleenex from her bag to blow her nose.

"Listen, Cody told me something."

"Chris, I really have to—"

"He told me you still love me."

Sara wiped her eyes and turned around to face him. "Maybe you should listen to him. Maybe you should listen to both of us, Chris."

Chris nodded. "I'm trying."

"I've gotta go. Feel better."

"Okay," he replied meekly, but she was already gone.

14. AN OFFICERS' DINNER

The officers' dining room was on the mountain above Senbruch. The lights of the camp sprawled out below; the yards deserted, the barracks dark shapes in the night, except when the spotlights washed over them with blinding yellow light.

Tonight was a special night. The SS had invited the regular guard detail to dinner.

Hans sat among them, among the dark gods who always smelled of blood. He smiled and laughed, smiled and laughed as the officers told their stories and jokes: "We raped the Jewish bitch right there on the street," and "We kicked the old dog until he coughed up blood." The guard detail made hogs of themselves, consuming huge amounts of the fine meats and wine. Most of them were drunk.

Herr Streche tapped his champagne glass with his spoon. He smiled with charm at the small crowd.

Hans could smell the blood off of his tongue and lips as he opened his mouth to speak, see it caked beneath Streche's manicured fingernails. And yet he smiled, because smiling was expected.

Herr Streche continued to tap his glass until the crowd quieted down.

"Gentlemen, you may have wondered why we have gathered you here tonight." Herr Streche paused and licked his ruby lips. His smile disappeared and his pupils narrowed to dagger points. "It is to prove a point," he said slowly.

With this, he rose and walked over to the window. "Down there," he said, pointing to the camp, "is our war. We officers of the SS believe a war is won by discipline.

Senbruch is not a camp, gentlemen. Senbruch is discipline!" With this he slammed his jeweled fist onto the table.

He began to walk down the table. "Are you ready to win this war, Muller? Are you, Geisthardt?" he questioned the guards.

Herr Streche stopped behind Hans' chair. His large hands gripped Hans' shoulders and his fingers dug into Hans' flesh like talons. Hans could feel the warm, bloodied breath on his neck.

"Are you, Herr Richter? Are you ready to win this war of discipline?"

Sweat broke out on Hans' forehead. Out of the periphery of his vision he could see Streche's ceremonial dagger. *If only...just a little closer...*

"Ja woll, Herr Streche," Hans quipped.

"Please speak up, Hans! Why you are not a kleine mouse running up a grandfather clock! ARE YOU READY TO WIN THIS WAR OF DISCIPLINE?"

"JA WOLL!" Hans barked, rising out of his chair.

"Excellent!" exclaimed Herr Streche, slapping him on the back. "We must all be ready," he said, returning to the head of the table. The other officers smiled at them fiercely. "We must all be ready, because our war in not with France, or Russia, or Britain. It is with the Jews."

Herr Streche returned to his seat. He paused for a second and watched the hands of his gold pocket watch turn.

"The work detail from Block 32 was late today. While you are in here dining, some of my men are down there winning the war."

A gunshot echoed off the mountainside.

All eyes turned towards the window.

There was another report.

The officers began to laugh. The guards, uncertain but certain they must act, began to laugh with them.

There were three more shots in rapid succession.

The officers' laughter had turned into low thunder and the guards' giggles into high-pitched shrieks.

More shots sounded below, and Hans, smelling the blood on the air, laughed with them.

15. GIRL AFRAID

She was afraid. She tried to ball up her fists against her eyes so she would not have to see, but her red curly hair got in the way and made her face itch.

She was afraid of the cold piece of metal against her head. She knew it made a loud *bang!* and then a red gush, and then it made people dead.

Her feet fumbled uncertainly in the darkness, but the man pushed her forward, sometimes carrying her by the back of her collar.

She did not know the hallway beyond her cell. She counted the bare light bulbs as they passed overhead—one, two, three, four.

The other children stopped talking as they passed. They would move back against the walls of their cells and try to make themselves flat. Some could not be silent; the fluid in their lungs spoke for them in hacking barks.

Hans hated that sound. He heard it in his sleep. He heard it high above on the mountain above Senbruch. He heard it within the black wheels of the trains that crated in the Jews and he heard it echo throughout the woods which surrounded the camp.

At this moment more than any other, he wished he could not hear it.

The pair came to a large steel door protected by a guard.

"Pass, bitte."

Hans held his breath as he held up the forgery.

"Where are you taking the child?" the guard asked in German.

"Herr Streche has ordered me to dispose of her in the woods. He says that for every Jewish girl we kill now there will be one less Jewish bitch to deal with later."

The girl began to whimper.

The guard turned and unlocked the heavy door. "Heil Hitler!"

"Heil Hitler," Hans replied.

The door closed heavily behind them. It was cooler in this part of the tunnel, but the stench of urine and excrement that hovered around the cells was gone, replaced by the heady smells of the forest.

Hans holstered his Luger. "Do not be afraid," he whispered to the girl, taking her hand. She sniffled and rubbed her eyes, refusing to look at him.

The passageway sloped gradually upwards. Hans had learned to love this part of the trip, when the checkpoint was far behind him and nature filled his senses. It tasted like freedom. Freedom for this girl. Freedom for all of the children of Senbruch.

They reached a slotted metal door. Hans reached behind the swastika banner to his right and pulled down hard on a rusting lever. The door clicked open, revealing a short staircase. Sunlight danced down the steps.

Hans removed his Luger once again.

She began to scream and pound her small fists against his thigh, kicking and biting. He scooped her up under one arm.

"I will not hurt you!" he hissed.

Hans paused at the top of the stairway. He could hear birds in the trees and squirrels foraging in the underbrush, but nothing more. He stepped up into the daylight.

A soft rain had just fallen, adding freshness to the air. Spurs of golden sunlight fell through the trees. It was infinitely beautiful; it was infinite peace. Hans could not linger to enjoy it.

He ran through the forest, breathing heavily as he carried the girl. She had stopped crying.

They reached a sloping streambed. He knocked twice on the earth. "Freedom," he said.

As the girl's eyes widened, the earth began to shift and push upwards. Hans put one hand on the small door and helped muscle it open.

An old man was crouched down in the portal. He looked both frightened and hopeful.

"Hans! It is a miracle!"

Hans clasped his grandfather's hands. "Opa, I have brought another."

"A miracle," he repeated, his large weathered hands wrapping around the girl as Hans passed her to him.

"It is too few and too far between."

"It will be everything to her," the old man replied.

Hans sighed and handed his grandfather a scroll. They clasped hands once again. "For freedom, Opa."

"For freedom, Hans. I love you."

Hans nodded. "Quickly, now."

His grandfather winked and he and the girl disappeared into the earth, pulling the small rusty door shut behind them.

Hans scooped up mud and earth from the streambed and layered it over the door. He was quiet for a moment as he held both hands against it. "For freedom," he whispered to himself, then cautiously made his way back to Senbruch.

16. CODY'S BAND

The murmur of faculty and parents filled the small auditorium. Chris was nervous. He had never been big on PTA or other school-related events before the separation, and he didn't quite know how to act among the strangers. He meandered over to the punch bowl, hoping to find Sara in the small crowd.

"Mr. Burton?" a low voice inquired.

"Yes?" Chris replied.

A large, bald-headed man stood before him. He extended his hand. "I'm Coach Peters. Your boy Cody is one of my students."

"Nice to meet you," Chris responded, gripping the man's hand in return.

"Frankly, you don't seem the type."

"Come again?" Chris asked.

"You know, Big Wig, Wheeler-Dealer type. Cody can't stop talking about how successful you are at your financial firm."

Chris turned the shade of an apple. "Cody sometimes exaggerates." <u>He really, really can exaggerate</u>, Chris thought to himself.

"Well, I know how bad you must feel about missing so many of his activities. You don't get these years again, I know. Hell, mine is already grown-up and married."

"Yeah, it's hard."

"Well, best of luck to him. He's a fine boy. What does he play? Clarinet?"

"Yes, I believe so." Chris had no idea.

"Fine instrument. Enjoy the show," Mr. Peters said.

"Yes, a pleasure to meet you."

"You also," Mr. Peters shouted as he pushed his way towards the bake sale table. Chris felt like putting his face in the punch bowl.

"Chris!" a woman cried.

Oh no, not again. Chris turned around and was speechless. The most beautiful woman he had ever seen stood before him. Her blue eyes penetrated his soul, her long blonde hair fell in curls around her bare shoulders, which contrasted pleasantly with her shimmering mauve evening dress.

"Sara, you look wonderful."

"Wow, I should drag this rag out more often. I can't remember the last time you told me that."

"You do, really gorgeous."

"Should we find our seats?" she asked, extending her arm. The band had begun the painstaking task of tuning their instruments.

They walked down the aisle, arms linked together. Some of the teachers whispered and pointed as they passed.

Chris turned his head and glared back at them.

"Oh, don't mind them," Sara told him. "They're just old school marms looking for gossip."

Chris burst out laughing. After regaining his composure, he whispered, "It's nice to be here with you."

Sara's blue eyes dazzled back at him.

They found seats near the front.

"Mom! Dad!" Cody yelled from the stage, waving his trumpet.

They stood up, waving and clapping.

The band began their first number, the squeaks and hoots and drum rolls all out of tune and time. The piece seemed to trudge along at its own ponderous pace endlessly.

"God," Chris whispered into Sara's ear, "they're really terrible!"

"Awful!" she giggled, putting her head on his shoulders.

"Sara, do you think that maybe—" Sara put a finger over his lips. "Shhhhhh."

Chris squeezed her tightly and she moved closer to him. They looked into each other's eyes, and found the love that had been damaged and tossed aside there.

It was meant to be a small kiss, but as they lingered on one another's lips it became deep and passionate.

"Really! Such antics should be left in the bedroom," a lady behind them scolded.

Chris turned his head, looked her square in the eyes, and replied calmly, "Up yours, lady."

Her face turned red with indignation.

They laughed and laughed. Cody smiled at them and waved during the number, his mouth still pressed to the mouthpiece of the trumpet.

To them, this band was suddenly the best thing they had ever heard.

Finally, the piece sputtered and whined into its crescendo. There was a *crack!* of two wood blocks from the percussion section.

"Oh no," Chris moaned, feeling a familiar pain at his temples...

It is late autumn. The leaves on the trees surrounding the camp have turned into beautiful hues of fire, fire that the prisoners could not touch but yet warmed them anyway.

They were coming.

Hans Richter could hear the Allies crashing through the southern forests, could hear the screams in Dresden as firestorms swept the city, could see his country's cathedrals fall into blackened ruin. And although these things broke his heart, he kept on smiling.

For they were coming for the children.

There are gallows on the assembly field of the Senbruch concentration camp. Hans Richter waited on the platform with a noose around his neck.

Herr Streche was barking at him, but he was oblivious to it: "You have been accused of having turned against the Reich and the Fuhrer! How do you plead?" Hans could smell the blood on Streche's breath. But they were coming for him and the others. Soon it would be Streche's own blood on his lips.

Hans did not reply.

"Dog!" spat Streche. "Hang him," he said coldly to the executioner.

Hans studied the faces of the guards and officers gathered on the assembly field. Their faces were full of contempt. Hans smiled at them, going down the whole line until each man met his gaze.

The floor disappeared beneath his feet and the noose tightened around his neck, and he kept on smiling.

17. A LETTER FROM THE UNIVERSITY

Dear Mr. Burton,

My name is Professor Brecht. I am the professor of Germanic studies at James Madison University. Our mutual friend, George Kushner, forwarded your scroll on to me for translation.

First, let me say that the scroll appears to be authentic. Aging analysis has been performed and has conclusively dated the scroll to fifty three years of age, meaning that it was produced sometime in 1943. With the help of a colleague overseas, I was also able to locate the author's military record, which further verifies the validity of the document. I did not forward the piece itself due to its rarity. It is indeed a fascinating find—perhaps you would be willing to let me hold onto it for research purposes? The requirements for getting tenure around here are tougher than ever.

In any case, I thought you would appreciate a written translation of the scroll:

My name is Hans Richter. I am twenty-three years of age this day.

I am a soldier of the Ninth German Army. I have fought in Czechoslovakia and Poland. I helped drive the British back to the coast of France. I have seen many men die (some in combat, others in quieter circumstances). I am accustomed to war and I see it as a man's duty to fight for his nation. No man loves Germany more than I, not even Adolf Hitler.

It is with sorrow but necessity that I write this note.

In the summer of 1942 I was transferred to the Senbruch concentration camp in southern Germany. In the summer of 1942 I was transferred to hell. This camp is beyond war, beyond friend or enemy, beyond God or the devil. The camp is death, and myself and comrades-in-arms are its keepers. There is no glory in this killing, no military victory—only cowardice and defeat for all involved.

There are tunnels beneath the Senbruch concentration camp—stone corridors which stretch out into endless darkness.

The tunnels are for the children. They grow up here, not like children but like moles—hairless and pale, bloated with starvation.

Hitler's doctors come to these children. They open their cells and take them away to their laboratories. The children return not as human children but as monsters. They have scars that show horrible probings and invasion. Many have had lobotomies. These poor souls are already as good as dead. They will never live or love as human beings.

I have shot several of these children. I tell my comrades it is because of my hatred for the Jews, but it is for mercy.

It is for these children that I fight. I can do little for the adults in the barracks. They are carefully counted at morning parade and assigned to work details. If they begin to disappear, many will be slaughtered in retribution. Through the children I must breathe onto the light of hope for the Jewish people.

During my two years I have delivered twenty-five children to safety. There is much more work to be done before the war's end.

If this child has successfully escaped Germany then this note is in the hands of a citizen of one of the Allied nations.

Bring this note to your newspapers, your radio announcers, your leaders and your generals. This is my message to them: Invade from France. Join with the Russians and invade also from the east. Run up Italy's boot and drive a fatal stake into the heart of my beloved country. The evil of this empire must end.

Liberate Senbruch.

Free the children.

Hans Richter
Soldier for the children

EPILOGUE

The shops and homes of the Jews are deserted. The dark trains rumble endlessly through the desolate, wasted land, at once going everywhere and nowhere. The sky overhead is filled with spirits who wish to weep like the rain but cannot.

There is a meager light that sheds illumination over the black tracks. Looking closer, one can see that a single menorah burns through the long night. It is hope. It is the combined strength of all persecuted peoples.

It is for the six million spirits who hover in the sky over Germany, and it still guides their way through the darkness in our time.

HAARTH THE HUNTER

By

R. David Fulcher

It was not a large castle. Its small, offset tower barely broke the tree line of the Black Forest. The red, white, and black standards hanging by the gate twisted in the autumn breeze as guards patrolled the battlements, their boots clicking on the ancient stone. When the moonlight fell through the trees at just the right angle, one could dimly make out the white SS runes on their collars and the dull gleam that reflected off of the barrels of their submachine guns.

The night air was filled with the chanting of an old and evil mantra, and for a moment the footsteps paused. The voices rose and fell, a guttural cascade that chilled the blood in its antiquity and primordial rhythms. It reverberated off of the stone walls, seeming to come from everywhere at once. The guards exchanged glances silently, afraid to guess at the nature of the experiments taking place below. They had witnessed many unnamable things since their assignment to Wewelsburg, and this too would be forgotten except in nightmare.

Within the castle walls, orange demon eyes could be seen from the tower windows opening and closing in time with the bonfires within. The tower itself was partially in ruin. The spiraling steps which once reached its height had since crashed to the tower floor, and stars could be seen through a large hole in the tower's ceiling.

The scene appeared misplaced in time. Perhaps it would not have been out of place at the monoliths at Stonehenge, or in ancient Sumeria. But in wartime Nazi Germany it was unique.

Figures stood rigidly around the fire, with runes painted on their faces and broad daggers hanging off of sashes that cinched their black robes sharply at the waist. They were the source of the chant, seven voices speaking as one.

The leaves in the courtyard were struck by a sudden wind, springing up and dancing in funnel patterns like whirling dervishes.

The earth tore open. One brown, muscular arm broke free from the dirt followed by another, each long enough to crush a deer in its curl. Spotlights from the battlements swung onto the disturbance.

"Achtung! Feuer!" Staccato flashes of light erupted across the battlements as the guards poured bullets into the courtyard. One of the arms hurled a chunk of earth the size of a motorcycle at the battlements directly over the gate, sending guards tumbling off in all directions.

A figure burst forth from the tower waving his arms. "Halt!" he cried, "Halt!" He looked ghastly in his robes and face paint under the glare of the spotlights.

"Halt!" repeated the captain of the guard, and all were still.

One by one, the robed men from the tower filed out into the courtyard. The last three carried something long and heavy.

The first robed man stepped forward to address the guards. The man-like thing in the courtyard reared its frame to its full height, and now its head was even with the castle walls. The guards raised their guns once again but the robed figure held up his hand in protest.

"Dieses Abend, du hast einen Gott gesehen."

(This night, you have seen a god)

"Ein Gott fur Das Reich."

(A god for the Reich)

"Er ist als uns, a waffe fur Deutschland."

(He is like us, a weapon for Germany)

The last three robed figures carried their burden forward into the light. They were carrying links of heavy gold chain.

The leader once again began the incantations, and the chain bearers followed him cautiously as he approached the giant.

Antlers rose through the coarse hair on the giant's head, and a wicked blade hung from his hips. It had a deer's head of human-like expression and carriage.

The giant bowed his head, and the robed leader beckoned the chain bearers forward. Nervously they lifted the heavy chain over the points of the creature's horns and around its thick neck. Once the chain was in place, the chain bearers scurried back to the safety of the castle walls.

The creature stood, majestic in its defiant strength. Like a small star, an eagle hung on its chest, and in its talons a swastika.

* * *

The U.S. Army's 42nd Rainbow Division slept fitfully that night. Snow had settled deep and white over the heart of the fatherland, an enemy more tenacious than the remnants of the Wehrmacht which had battled over every hedgerow in France and sniped at them from every burnt-out building and farmhouse.

On nights such as this the jeeps and tanks were kept running all night so that the engine fluids would not freeze. Men who could not sleep would pop the hoods of the jeeps and warm their hands over the engines, trying to bring sensation back into their fingers.

One of these men was Sergeant Drake of the 5th Recon Squadron. He paced back and forth in the brittle dark like a caged panther, occasionally jumping up and down or jogging in place for warmth.

It was not the cold that kept him awake. Drake and the other men had long since grown accustomed to that. In a strange way, it was like the killing. You would prefer to live without it, but if that was not possible you could teach yourself to forget. At least for a little while.

It was anxiety that kept him awake. Tomorrow they would break camp and take over for 7th Recon, who for two weeks had been out on patrol twenty miles ahead of the front.

The Germans would never surrender, Drake knew this much. Their fanaticism exceeded that even of the Japanese. Old men and young children awaited them in far off Berlin, a rag tag army in ill-fitting uniforms but still an army, willing to kill and die for the Reich. This, if nothing else, made them dangerous.

The regular army units were in retreat. Rumor had it that a major counter-offensive was brewing behind the lines, one final gambit to toss the Allied advance back to the sea.

Sergeant Drake was a man that placed his bets on gut instincts. The survivors—excluding those that were simply lucky–were the same way. His guts were upset this night, warning him that trouble awaited the 5th in the skirling snow and the hard days ahead.

Pacing back and forth, back and forth, his breath crystallizing in the cold night air, he placed his numb hands once again over the coughing and spitting engine of the jeep.

<u>Maybe there is a Jerry bullet with my name on it</u>, he thought without any real emotion. <u>Perhaps then I will finally get some sleep.</u>

Perhaps then I will be warm, he thought.

*   *   *

Private Johnson of the 7th Recon Squadron was not a good night watch. He was a nervous wreck, a paranoid living on a hair trigger. The men of the 7th hated putting Johnson on guard duty, but they hated missing sleep more. So like the others Johnson took his shift.

Johnson pulled his jacket closer, hoping to keep out the chill wind which swept through the surrounding trees and caused the frozen branches to click together like bones. He knew somebody was watching him. He darted his head about furiously trying to see everywhere at once.

There it was again—the snapping of twigs and movement in the brush that sounded uncomfortably close to the camp. He hesitated before waking the others. He had already awakened the men once when he saw that awful silhouette on the hill, the silhouette that resembled a deer but could not have been a deer because deer don't walk around upright like men. They had pelted him with jokes before going back to sleep: "Johnson is seeing Jerry again!" and "No more rations for Johnson!"

Movement. Johnson's stomach knotted and he held his breath. Something was out there, something close, he was sure now.

He would have screamed when he felt the hot animal breath on his neck, would have screamed but for the blade which cut through his jugular.

Private Johnson gave up his spirit easily, and the Hunter released the limp body as its lifeblood painted the snow crimson. Mercifully, the others were slain in their sleep, perhaps dreaming sunlit visions of love, home, and happiness before succumbing to death.

Haarth the Hunter was efficient. Each man was strung up and gutted. None of the precious meat was wasted.

* * *

Sergeant Drake dropped to the ground, his face stinging in the fallen snow. Jarkowski, the man in front, was already dead or dying, and there was no way the Doc could reach him under the steady stream of fire from the German MG 42. If there were more than the two firing and feeding the machine gun, they were under cover or successfully camoflauged into the forest. Drake had to move the unit or the Germans would move forward and finish them off as they remained hopelessly pinned down by the suppressive fire.

If it was only the machine gun crew in the area, his unit would have to flank their position.

Suddenly the gun went silent. Drake listened. He could hear the snowflakes falling, and he cursed himself for his slowness in recognizing what was happening.

"Fire in the hole!" he yelled, springing forward and sprinting towards a line of pines to the right. Out of the corner of his eye he saw his men diving away in all directions, and then the German potato masher grenade spiraling end over end through the air towards their position.

The blast sent snow and dirt high into the air. Drake used the distraction to take cover to the right of the machine gun nest and draw his rifle level. The machine gun feeder raised his head and Drake sent a round through his helmet. This enraged his comrade, who once again opened up with the machine gun. The rest of 5th squadron, now entrenched and in positions of advantage, returned fire.

The machine gun stopped barking, and Drake could hear the German cursing as he desperately tried to clear a jam. Reynolds, one of faster men, managed to navigate his way through the trees and behind the German's position. A minute later the German emerged from the nest, his hands held high. Reynolds kept the muzzle of his M1 hard against the prisoner's neck as he walked him out.

"Doc!" bellowed Drake, but he hadn't needed to yell. Doc was already at Jarkowski's side attempting to staunch the gaping wound in his chest. Jarkowski spasmed violently and a trail of blood ran out of the corner of his mouth. He did not move again.

Doc knelt down beside him and closed his eyelids. He ripped off Jarkowski's dog tags and checked the ammo pouch on his waist. It snapped open like a coffin in the thin air. The Doc removed a small metal cross from the pouch and placed it on Jarkowski's chest. Doc had taken over the religious duties after the squadron's Chaplain had been killed during the Normandy landings.

"Goddamn Krauts," hissed Bernstein, "goddamned no good Krauts!"

Reynolds poked the prisoner in the back with his muzzle. "Do you want me to do him, Sarge?" he asked.

"No," answered Drake, whose guts were aching something terrible.

All eyes turned on him in accusation. "No?!?" asked Reynolds in disbelief.

"I said no. We might need him."

"For what?" Bernstein countered angrily.

"I don't know, Jack," Drake muttered, scanning the snow-covered hills. "I really don't know."

* * *

The Hunter smelled blood on the wind, down in the valley below near the place where he had killed seven of the man-things while they had slept.

His thigh pulsed with pain where a stone from one of the man-thing's fire sticks had struck him on the night of his resurrection.

He had learned to trust his senses to locate the man-things when they hid themselves in white skins in the snow. He could hear them in the trees, their slow even breathing like the movement of a small bird in flight, and beneath that the smell of the dark red juice that warmed him like no other nourishment.

Initially, he would wait for the ones in grey, those that wore the strange hacked cross rune on their coverings and spoke in a language which had roots in the ancient tongue of his race. He would wait for them, but for reasons he could not understand he would not slay them, so he had learned to hide from them and hunt the man-things in the green coverings in their place.

But the men in the green coverings were few, and the Hunter once again needed flesh and red juice to warm him on the winter slopes.

Using his massive arms, the Hunter pushed aside the stone and bark that concealed his lair and rose up, his breath pluming from his flaring nostrils in serpentine threads.

He waited.

He waited until he could hear the distant streams running under the skim of ice and the clicking talk of the frozen pine branches, sounds that spoke to him more clearly than the speech of the man-things.

He waited until he was sure that in this place there was only himself and the eternal hum of the forest.

Then Haarth followed new blood.

* * *

Sergeant Drake halted the company by a small stream.

He motioned to Bernstein to take point and Hickman to take rearguard.

Reynolds put the muzzle against the prisoner's cheek and put a finger over his lips to command silence.

Drake unslung his pack and removed the leather pouch that contained the maps. He studied them a moment to confirm his suspicions. The base camp of 7th Squadron should be right over the next hill. Although no one had said it, they all expected the worse. Hickman had tried to raise the sergeant of 7th Squadron several times by radio without success.

Snowflakes fell onto the map and melted, making new towns and rail junctions in small dark circles of moisture. Drake motioned to Hickman to attempt to raise 7th Recon again.

"Lost dogs to kennel, lost dogs to kennel, come in kennel."

There was only static and the near-silent run of stream water beneath ice. Drake called the men to him.

"All right boys, I expect the worse. Jerry may have gotten the best of 7th Squadron, but they won't get the best of the 5th."

"I want all of you to assume flanking positions from one another ten yards apart. Base camp should be right over the next rise. Check your rifles, and Reynolds, cover that Kraut!"

When they crested the hill, Sergeant Drake witnessed several events at once: Reynolds striking the jaw of the German prisoner. Hickman bent over and vomiting. Bernstein clasping the Star of David around his neck and praying.

The scene which faced the men of the 5th was one from a nightmare. The base camp was covered in blood; it slicked the firewood and made obscene lines across the canvas pup tents; it fed the stream amber wine and made bleak snow angels of death in the light powder.

A haphazard pile of greenish-brown tubing was frozen together in the middle of the camp like a grotesque monument. It was the intestines. Above it all was the smell of rotting meat from the pink carcasses of men that creaked and swung like hooked cattle from the trees.

Drake grabbed the prisoner by the collar and pulled him up from the ground where he had been nursing his bruised jaw.

"Was hast du getun!" he demanded, shaking the enemy soldier.

(What have you done!)

The prisoner rapidly shook his head back and forth in negation.

"Nein! Nicht uns. Es war Der Jager!"

(No! Not us. It was The Hunter!)

"Wo ist Der Jager? Soltner? SS?" Drake persisted.

(Who is The Hunter? Soldier? SS?)

"Nein! Der Jager ist ein Mann-Tier. Der Jager ist ein Gott!"

(No! The Hunter is a man-animal. The Hunter is a god!)

Drake spat into the German's face and threw him back to the ground. Reynolds lowered his rifle over his head but Drake pushed it aside.

"What happened?" asked Doc.

"I wish I knew, Doc. He's not talking sanely. He told me it wasn't they that did this, but something called 'The Hunter'."

"SS?" countered Doc.

"No. I asked him."

"He's lying, Sarge," quipped Hickman, "let's beat the truth out of him."

The others nodded in agreement.

"No one is going to touch him without going through me." The men looked at one another with uncertainty. "We have a job to do for the U.S. Army, and part of that job is bringing prisoners back to Intelligence for interrogation. *Live* prisoners."

"We have our orders, and until I hear otherwise we are going to follow them. We will bivouac here tonight."

The men cursed and grumbled, but eventually dispersed and went about their tasks.

"Reynolds, cut down those men and recover their dog tags. The rest of you take down those tents and burn them along with any other gear you find. You have your orders—now move out!"

* * *

The recon patrol began at dawn the next morning. They had gagged the prisoner the night before after giving him some K rations and water.

Drake was taking point. Their progress was slow as they were patrolling inside the operational zone of the Wehrmacht. It was around noon that they struck the jackpot.

If the sun had been at a different angle, Drake would have missed the small gleam which shone above the forest floor.

Calling the company to a halt, Drake signaled for silence. The reflector shone again. After advancing silently down the valley towards the source for an hour the outline of a rough airstrip could be made out. Training his field glasses across the strip, Drake located the source of the strange reflector—a long, sloping nose, two cylindrical jet turbines hanging like fat bats from short wings, and a bubble canopy. It was a camouflaged German Me 262 jet fighter.

Drake had been shown photos of this new German super weapon during briefings, but he had never thought that he would encounter one. More surveying of the field revealed a small barracks at the opposite end.

A ground crewman motored towards the plane on a small car with a 500 kg bomb in tow. The prisoner made muffled grunts in a weak attempt to get the crewman's attention, but was quickly subdued by Reynolds.

A German MG 34 on a tripod across from the barracks pointed up at the sky for light flak support.

Drake motioned Hickman over to the gun. Hickman silently tracked through the woods to the opposite end of the clearing. Drake held up one hand to signal the others to hold their positions, then he disappeared after Hickman.

Pausing in the woods near the sleek fighter, Drake watched as the mechanic prepared the bomb rack under the fuselage for the next mission. Drake stole forth from the woods and cracked the mechanic across the neck with the butt of his pistol. The mechanic dropped and Drake crouched down low beneath the wing and covered the mechanic's body with snow. Drake watched the windows and waited as forms moved back and forth within the barracks.

Although Drake could not see Hickman, he knew Hickman was in position and ready to move.

Emerging from cover, Drake raised his hand and thrust it down quickly. Hickman emerged from the woods and manned the machine gun. As he snapped back the bolt on the MG, Drake pulled the pin on a grenade and tossed it under the plane. He then sprinted back to the woods.

There was a huge explosion as the jet fuel combusted, sending burning hunks of debris high into the blue sky. Hickman mowed down the pilot and ground crew as they emerged from the barracks.

Drake motioned him forward and Hickman stepped over the dying men to toss a grenade into the barracks.

There was a second explosion and rain of debris and then nothing more but the crackling of burning wood.

* * *

The Hunter paused in his journey, stunned by flames which shot straight up into the sky. He had been following the smell of new blood down into the valley. He waited, and then there was another sound like a thousand trees breaking at once, and more fire. It reminded him of the fire at the strange stone place where he was raised so many nights before. Up ahead, a fire stick was shouting, and he could smell blood commingled with smoke and gasoline.

The Hunter felt weak. He had tried to work out the stone in his thigh at the stream, rubbing his flank against bark, but that only caused more pain and re-opened the wound. Now he was confused, enraged by pain, and unconsciously saddened by the unspoken will that commanded him relentlessly forward.

* * *

Drake's guts began to ache on the way back to base camp. First it was a mild upset, his bowels disagreeing with the spam-like mixture that made up his K rations, and then it progressed to the tell-tale ache of trouble.

Drake halted the march, raising his hand for silence. There was only the sound of his own heartbeat and Reynolds chomping on an unlit Lucky Strike cigarette. Drake looked over in annoyance, and paused in horror as blood beaded out of Reynolds' mouth around the butt of the cigarette.

Reynolds was hefted off of his feet, and the tip of a blade became visible through the fabric of his uniform. It tore upwards to his breast bone, almost cutting him in half before the blade slipped out and the body was dropped to the ground like an empty husk.

"Kill it!" Drake shouted, raising his pistol to aim between the creature's eyes. The pistol was slapped out of his hand and he was thrown hard to the earth. The German prisoner pinned him down, grinning fiendishly. Drake kicked him in the groin, and he fell aside groaning.

Around Drake the scene was chaos. Doc was walking towards the beast, holding up a cross in defiance, quoting the Lord's prayer: "Our father, who art in heaven, hallowed be thy name..." The creature easily batted Doc away with a massive fist, sending him sliding down a rocky slope.

Hickman charged the creature with his bayonet. The Hunter sensed his approach, and swung his blade in a backward arc which cut Hickman across the throat in a crimson spray.

Bernstein, who had been on point, burst through the brush to see what was happening and smacked into the creature's chest. Stunned, he backed up in disbelief at the malformed head that glared down at him with black eyes.

The Hunter raised his blade.

Bernstein held his rifle above his head to deflect the blow, and the serrated edge cut through the barrel in a shower of sparks and cut him from shoulder to ribs.

During their combat Drake recovered his pistol from the snow and pulled the prisoner to his feet. He placed his pistol at the German's temple.

He tried to ignore the dead and dying around him, who this time were not faceless enemies but *his* men, *his* old friends.

The Hunter, its furred chest drenched in blood, faced Drake. It was confused. The man-thing was rabid, dangerous—he could sense that. He held another man-thing in front of him, a man-thing with a grey covering, a taboo man-thing.

The man-thing continued to advance, and the Hunter's brain became red with fear. With nowhere else to turn, the instinct to survive took over. The Hunter lowered his massive frame and buried the jagged points of his antlers deep into his adversary's human shield, hoping to slay them both.

Drake stepped back and released the writhing prisoner, and the massive tines of the Hunter's antlers ripped through the prisoner's back as he screamed. The Hunter snorted in anger and swung his head wildly, throwing the carcass free and down the slope.

Then they were alone, two timeless hunters against the backdrop of the forest. The Hunter could not move, paralyzed by uncertainty. He had done wrong by killing the man-thing in the grey covering, and feared retribution from the sky gods.

In a moment Drake drew a bead on the creature's skull. The Hunter evaded, but a second too late. The bullet blew out the Hunter's right eye and became lodged in the bone.

The Hunter's alien, shrill cry of pain reverberated across the mountains. He kicked his legs wildly, his hooves throwing a shower of snow as he thrust his fists blindly at this dangerous man-thing. Drake stumbled backward, having lost his wind from the rain of blows that fell across his torso.

Rolling over, he fired his pistol into the snowy mist, but the Hunter was gone.

* * *

Doc came to.

His curly hair was crisp with frost. He tried to sit up, and winced in pain at the effort. A small pine had stopped his fall down the mountainside, and the impact with it had bruised his ribs.

Slowly, he stood up. He recognized the path some fifty yards above. After a slippery, perilous journey up to the path he discovered the bodies of Reynolds, Hickman, and Bernstein. He closed their eyelids and placed crosses over their chests. If time permitted, he would bury them. He found no trace of the Sarge, and this provided him with a glimmer of hope as he patrolled the area.

Doc removed Reynolds' .45 from its holster, its weight feeling odd in his untrained hands.

Now there were devils among the armies of men, and Doc was on a holy mission.

*   *   *

Splinters of ice flew into the air as the Hunter brought his hooves down into the stream bed. He grabbed a chunk of the broken ice and jammed it into his hollow eye socket. There was fire in his head, deeper fire than that which had been in his leg, but the ice would briefly numb it.

He had made a mistake fleeing the man-thing that fought like an animal. It was wrong to fear any man-thing, no matter how powerful. They were provided by the gods for nourishment. He would have to partake of this warrior's flesh to make things right. Perhaps then the sky gods would smile upon him and remove the fire in his head. Perhaps then they would make him truly free, like his kind had always been free to run through the forested hills of Europe. Perhaps then they would remove the alien will and thoughts from his head that drove him ever onwards on some unknown course.

*   *   *

Drake looked down at the base camp. The clearing betrayed no trace of the recent massacre, save for a few deep nicks in the large branches that overhung the camp area. His men had been thorough in burning down all traces of the recent atrocity, as if attempting to burn it from their memories as well. They were now dead. Drake would still have to live with it.

Somewhere below the Hunter was waiting for him, and he was ready to end it.

It had been a day, a night, and another half-day since 5th Squadron's encounter with the Hunter, and Drake now carried a bullet in his right leg where a Panzer grenadier unit had fired on him in the valley.

He had subsisted on snow and bark, but hunger gnawed at him like an ugly dwarf, adding to his wild appearance.

There was the sound of ice breaking violently somewhere below, and Drake limped down to the lonely arena. The Hunter was drinking from the stream when Drake found him. Drake carried his pistol and a small entrenchment tool he had found at the camp.

It would be a fair fight.

The Hunter, sensing his presence, lifted his gargantuan head from the stream, the muscles in his neck bunching and knotting with the motion. The Hunter turned to face this wild man-thing which emanated no fear scent.

Sizing one another up, the challengers waited. The Hunter removed his blade, and Drake hefted the entrenchment tool, and they began to circle in the timeless pose of warriors. Several birds flew out of the trees in anticipation of the coming violence.

Drake feinted a step in towards the Hunter, and the Hunter took the bait, swinging strongly for his head. Drake ducked, and planted the entrenchment tool's tip into the Hunter's empty eye socket. Snorting and stomping with rage, the Hunter stepped back and pulled the weapon free. The fire which the ice had all but extinguished was raging once again.

Sunlight reflected off of the golden eagle and swastika talisman that hung from the Hunter's neck, temporarily blinding Drake. He stepped back quickly, and when his vision was restored, the Hunter was wielding both his blade and the entrenchment tool and closing fast.

Drake punched him square in the snout. "Son of a bitch," he spat.

The blow stunned the Hunter, and Haarth stumbled back in surprise.

The combat had taught the Hunter that you could pretend to strike, and then move or attack more fiercely from another direction. As nothing had ever dared challenge him before, this was great knowledge.

The Hunter swung at Drake's head. Drake ducked, but something was terribly wrong. He did not hear the swish of air as the blade passed by. The Hunter had feinted the blow with his blade, and directed the strong attack at Drake's right leg with the entrenchment tool.

It was Drake's turn to feel fire. The bullet wound re-opened, and his leg grew warm with blood. He dropped to his knees.

The Hunter advanced, his blade raised over his head.

Sergeant Drake tried to find the sunset and hold the image in his mind before the blade fell.

Suddenly there was a loud report, and the Hunter paused, towering over him and swaying. It had a hole in its throat. There was another report, and a hole appeared in its forehead. Thick blood the color of mud began to escape the wounds as the Hunter stumbled around in a daze, swinging dumbly with its weapons at the air. Step forward, step back—now turn—the Hunter's death dance continued with agonizing grace.

Drake rolled aside as the Hunter thudded to the ground, shaking the snow from the tree limbs that had once supported its victims.

There was the snapping of twigs and underbrush, and Doc emerged from the woods with a .45 pistol in his hand.

"Doc, you old son of a bitch! I never would have guessed," Drake cajoled.

"Well, somebody's got to look out for you in this outfit."

"How did you know I would be here?"

"I didn't," Doc replied wryly. "Just following orders, Sarge. Regroup at base camp and all that."

Drake grinned. "You're one hell of a soldier, Doc."

"Thanks, but I think I'll stick to medicine. How's that leg?"

"Been better, been worse," Drake replied.

Doc nodded.

"You shouldn't have interfered, though. I had it under control."

"Yeah, right," Doc muttered, cutting Drake's pants below the thigh to reveal the wound.

"What happened to you out there, Doc? I thought you were a man of God. Good will towards others and all that. Even the birds and fish in the sea."

"Indeed, every creature that creepeth upon the earth. I'll never understand the killing of men. But that," he said, pointing at the Hunter's carcass, "is the closest thing to the devil I've seen on this earth."

"Did you see the necklace, Doc?" Drake asked. Doc nodded and kept working on wrapping the wound with a makeshift bandage. "It looked like gold."

"Yes, it did. Indeed it did," he replied, not looking up from his task.

"How would you like to open up that church you've always been talking about back in the states? What do you say? Fifty-fifty split?"

"Amen," he answered, taking a small cross from his ammo pouch and placing it on the Hunter's chest.

BARBAROSSA DIARY

By

R. David Fulcher

The stream, driven high and fast by the melting snow of the Russian winter, rushed past the small farmhouse like a flash of quicksilver. Threads of smoke wafted up from the chimney, spreading in the soft spring breeze. A man watched from the window.

"So you are waiting for a story?" the man asked, his back to the young boy who restlessly fidgeted by the great oven in the center of the room.

"Yes! Tell me about the knights of England, or the cowboys in America."

The man turned towards the boy, his brow knitted and troubled.

He took several uneasy steps forward, a sort of off-step shamble as he dragged his bad leg along with the rest of his body. He sat down next to the boy on the warm brickwork of the fireplace and placed one hand firmly on the boy's shoulder.

"Why not a story about Russia?" the man asked.

"Russia? You mean about creatures in the Black Sea, or the fierce wolves of Siberia?"

"No, I mean a story that took place on fields such as these around us, in the streams such as the one that runs by the window. It is a story of terror in the night, and the strength of people together. In short, it is the story of my leg."

"Oh, I already know about that. The Nazis shot you during the Great Patriotic War," the boy said matter-of-factly.

"Oh really?" asked the man with feigned surprise, "and who are these Nazis?"

"You know, bad guys. They wore black capes and looked like skeletons!"

The woman in the corner of the room, who had been kneading bread, looked up at the man and boy, her smiling face dotted with flour. The man winked back at her.

"Yes, well, it does seem that you know quite a lot about these Nazis," the man said, "but did you know that I was a Nazi, Michael?"

Michael's eyes grew wide with surprise. He turned to the woman in the corner of the room.

"Oh mama, is it true?"

"I'm afraid so, Michael," the woman said without looking up, her face set in determination as she worked the dough with hard fingers.

The man retrieved his pipe from the windowsill, leaving the boy alone to absorb the information. He lit the pipe, and the familiar tang of cherry wood and tobacco filled the room. He watched the stream run its course, and waited for the boy to speak.

"Father, I would like to hear this story," the boy said quietly. The man smiled and returned to his seat beside the boy.

"It all began with that," the man said, pointing to the radio across the room which stood like a brown idol. "This was Hitler's message to the German people in late June of 1941: 'I decided again today to place the fate and future of the Reich and our people in the hands of our soldiers.'"

"Of course, I wasn't there to hear the message myself—I was crossing the border into Russia."

"You mean...you mean you came here as one of the skeleton-things to destroy Russia!"

"Not exactly. You see, Michael, the Nazis were not monsters—at least not in the sense that you're talking about—they were only men, and some day you will understand the power of ideas and their ability to drive one's thoughts. I was 21, and believed I was doing the right thing. I believed that Germany deserved the lands it had lost during the First World War, and believed that the German empire could climb as high as the glory that was Greece. It was what we all believed, because that was what we were taught. We were not taught the price of such pride; we were left out in the field to discover that for ourselves."

"So I said goodbye to my parents in Munich—oh yes, I had parents, just as yourself—and was assigned to the 9th Army of the Wehrmacht. I saw Russia for the first time through German eyes, wearing a German uniform, and bearing a German rifle." The man paused in contemplation as the fire crackled.

"The invasion day itself was almost too big to describe. I would almost call it glorious if I did not know now the evil it heralded. Imagine it, Michael! As far as the eye could see to the left and right soldiers were marching across the border. Bombers passed overhead, shadowing our columns and shaking the sky like thunder. Panzers streaked out ahead of us, kicking up a low cloud of dust, and beyond that lay the vast plain of Russia. My young imagination mistook that which was big for that which was right, as one who mistakenly takes the larger, paved road over the smaller, untrodden path. On that day I embraced the doctrine of strength, and my blood hummed with the eternal song of the soldier."

"What is wrong with the strong leading the weak? Is that not the way of the wolves?"

Suddenly the man grabbed the boy's arm and bent it towards the hot face of the oven. The man used his other hand to open the oven's door. The flames licked out of the oven's face like liquid demons. The boy's small muscles bunched and strained, but could not fight the strength of the man's grip. Slowly, slowly the tiny limb was pulled towards the fire.

"Stop! Don't! Please, don't!" wailed the boy.

"Friedreich!" screamed the woman, leaving her bread aside and racing over to the oven.

The man moved the boy's arm over the top of the fire for a second as the flames licked greedily upwards. Then he whipped the arm back.

Tears welled up in the boy's eyes and he began to rub his arm where his father had gripped it. The woman made a move towards her son, but the man held her back. Gently he closed the oven door.

"Natasha, please. It's all right. It's just a lesson."

The woman stopped moving forward but remained standing by her husband and son.

"Why—Why did you do that?" the boy asked sniffling.

"Because I am stronger. Is that not the way of the wolves?"

"We're not wolves!" the boy snapped angrily.

"That's right, we are human beings. Should we behave like wolves?"

The boy shook his head slowly, watching the flames in the oven with new respect. His father looked away and sucked on his pipe, making small rings float through the air. The woman ruffled the boy's hair and knelt down beside the man. "No more lessons, I can't take it!" she whispered. The man smiled and she went back to her work, leaving the father and son, storyteller and audience, alone.

"Shall I continue?" asked the man.

"Yes," the boy said quietly, for deep within himself he felt something beyond the heat of the fire. It was understanding.

The man's voice, raspy with smoke, flowed on.

"I was assigned to Army Group Center. Our job was to penetrate through the middle of Russia and take Moscow.

"At first it seemed that it would only be a matter of days. Our Luftwaffe decimated the Red Air Force on the ground before the Russians knew they were in a war. We marched into Russia unopposed, and the younger ones among us thought this was war."

Natasha came between the father and son to slide the dough she had worked into the oven. She wiped her hands on her apron and sat beside them.

"I was a young woman at the time," she began, "and knew of such matters only from books and the burnt-out buildings left from World War I. It seemed inconceivable at the time that the Germans had turned their war dogs against us. We were supposed to be allies. The day the Germans invaded we were shipping supplies across the German border to support their war effort. I remember thinking 'Why do they attack their allies? Is there no honor among these men?'

"But of course with such men as Goebbels, Himmler, and Goering—and of course Hitler himself—there was only Germany, the golden fatherland and its pride. Meanwhile, the blood of Germany's sons ran in pools greater than the Gulf of Finland, in rivers higher and darker than the Volga."

Michael seemed confused, and the man could see that he desperately wanted to understand.

"Some men, Michael," he continued, "are not satisfied with this." He opened his arms as if to embrace the room.

"They get the idea that food, friends, and family sustain a man, but do not make a man. To make a man one must have an army and the implements of war. Do you see the problem, Michael?"

Michael shook his head quickly back and forth in negation.

"Because of those few, the whole lot of us are ruined. We must arm ourselves against such leaders. Others then feel they must defend themselves against us. Eventually we are all armed to the teeth and only time stands between us."

The boy pushed himself closer to his father, cocking his head as if better hearing would make the ideas simpler. The father sucked on his pipe reflectively and looked to the window. The birds sang with the ecstasy of spring in the distant trees. The father realized this would all take time, but they had time. With the stream and the change of seasons as their timepiece, they had time.

"I came from Smolensk," Natasha said. "We visited there when you were ten. Do you remember?"

"I remember!" chimed Michael. "The walled city on the Dnieper. It was black and broken."

"It was not always so. Before the Great Patriotic War, it was a bustling commercial center. Smolensk was the junction point of five railways, and we sent goods all over Russia. Linens, carpets, bricks—even beer. There was a university which had been built after the first world war, and I had great hopes of attending there although my father's bricklayer salary did not permit it. I worked long days down at the factory, but it did not matter. My father bought me new hats on holidays, and my mother and I would walk down by the river and talk about men. As a young woman, Smolensk seemed like the center of the world, and it was for me."

"Fortunately, we were hundreds of miles from the border, and although we heard terrible stories of dive bombers which shrieked like demons and SS death squads, we went about our work and hoped that our army could hold the advance. Soon the bombers came, boldly in daylight, and left entire sections of our city burning into the night."

"Our factories quickly stopped working on civilian goods and switched over to the production of guns, tanks, and munitions. Often we worked sixteen-hour days, and the pressure was terrible. We could feel the hot breath of the German wolves upon our necks as daily news came from the front of our army's retreat. As the days rolled by and the bombs fell with increasing frequency it became obvious that the Germans would claim our city as their own."

Natasha turned away. The man noticed his wife's clenched teeth and the single tear which coursed down her cheek. He took up the tale.

"I have said that at the beginning Russian resistance was weak. But soon, as the Communist Party began swaying the people's will against the invaders, and as news came from Lithuania and Estonia of the horrific treatment of civilians by the SS resistance began to stiffen."

"I remember one night in particular. It was the night I finally began to think about the evil machine I was a part of.

"The attack occurred sometime after midnight. Our unit was lost and our heavy guns were bogged down in the muddy roads. I fell asleep listening to the campfire, and had begun to dream when I was awakened by the sound of machine gun fire. For several moments I lay listening, and then I slipped out of my bedroll and fumbled for my helmet and rifle in the dark. I strapped on my helmet and poked my head out of the canvas flaps of the tent. There were shouts, shadowy forms running about, and a quick sizzle as someone dumped water on to the campfire. I stood up and grabbed the shoulder of a passing man. 'Was ist los?' I asked quickly, and the man pointed to the anti-aircraft gun several hundred yards away. Golden bursts flashed from the muzzles of the quad 20mm cannons as the gunner swiveled them around. I looked up in disbelief."

"There, like white droplets under the pearl moon, were dozens of paratroopers. They swayed violently back and forth from their chutes and shouted out to each other in desperation. Occasionally a burst of orange would flash below the white umbrellas as the soldiers shot wildly at the camp. Between the intermittent bursts of gunfire I could hear the distant rumble of the Russian transport plane which had dropped its human cargo."

Michael's eyes were full of horror and fascination, and he held his breath.

"Obviously, it was a misplaced drop, and the condemned souls which hovered above in the darkness knew it. Despite their wild efforts to change their direction, they slowly filtered downwards toward the camp. I watched as one by one the animate forms jerked on the delicate strands which suspended them above the earth as they were hit. The paratroopers hit the ground like dead weights as their ivory chutes closed over them like soft coffins.

"One landed near me. I lifted the cloth which covered him. Blood poured out of his wounds on to the hungry soil. He drew ragged breaths, and his face was pale beneath his dark hair. With tortuous effort his trembling hand lifted his pistol from the dewy grass and turned it slowly towards me.

"I clicked off the safety on my rifle and shot him dead. I watched it all from outside of myself. Around me the men cheered and danced, and lifted the anti-aircraft gunner on to their shoulders. I never felt more out of place, more like a stranger. A hand came out of the darkness and slapped me on the back. I turned. 'Heil Hitler!' the man yelled, saluting me. His name was Tobias, and that night I learned to hate him."

"Why did you kill the paratrooper, father?"

Friedreich shook his head back and forth, his eyes transfixed on a memory only he could see. Natasha had seen these eyes before, eyes which spoke of night and fire and the endless wails of mortar.

She pulled Michael close. "Oh, Michael, they were terrible times for the whole world." She gently caressed the boy's face. A breeze entered the room like a spirit and stayed to listen.

"You are so young, Michael! So full of hope. The Nazis robbed me of my hope, my city—even my parents. But worst of all they stole my youth."

"I knew nothing but an absolute hatred for these men, this nation called Germany. Hatred is like a dragon, Michael, it steals away children while they sleep."

"Did you hate father?" asked Michael. Natasha reached out and grabbed Friedreich's hand, uniting the circle of three.

"Oh, I tried," she said, throwing Friedreich a wink. "But he was half-dead when we found him. And despite myself I could not hate this man, although the others wanted to kill him. On the field, we would have fought as mortal enemies. But I couldn't do it this way."

"Did you fight, mother?"

"We all fought the Nazis, Michael. Some of us fought on the production lines, others on the front. But we all fought—children, old men, women—all of us."

"And could they fight!" exclaimed Friedreich, his eyes blazing. "Hitler's greatest oversight was the strength of the Russian people. To think he could take it all, from the Ukraine to Siberia, and hold it under his belt! Embrace this soil, Michael, for it shall always belong to you and your people."

Michael's pulse quickened with his father's words. He could feel the heat of his father's breath upon his face.

"Excuse me, Herr Czar, but you were telling Michael about our fighting ability," interrupted Natasha.

"Of course, my dear. In the beginning it seemed as if there was no backbone to the Russians. Our panzers and motorized units took the brunt of the initial assault, and our dive bombers and fighters destroyed the Red Air Force on the ground and in the air. We rolled forward, encircling the Red Army at every position. The roads were full of Russian prisoners. Minsk fell, and then your mother's city, Smolensk. The Russians were surprised by our attack and had received no orders to fight back. The units of our Blitzkrieg moved quickly into Russia over bridges and highways with little difficulty.

"It all began to change towards the end of the summer. We were harried on every supply route, at every bridge and airbase. Large sections of railway were destroyed beyond use, and the North/South highway had been severed, forcing our trucks and artillery on to the muddy roads. Bands of Russian partisans roamed the swamps and forests, hitting our positions like hawks and then vanishing into the forests like phantoms. Our generals were used to fighting a direct war, and had no idea how to fight back against this invisible army. Slowly the civilian bands destroyed our rear while the Red Army grew strong on the front.

"We lost our invulnerability, and the chill fall rains penetrated our summer uniforms and chilled us to the bone. That winter was the coldest in half a century, and only the officers wore lined boots and topcoats. At its coldest it would reach almost fifty below zero."

"Brrrrrr," said Michael, rubbing his hands together by the oven.

"We got within ten miles of Moscow and our war machine went kaputt, as the Germans would say. We had lost our will to fight. I had been considering deserting for some time. When Marco, my best friend, froze to death during his midnight watch I could no longer bear to stay."

"Did you like being a soldier, father?"

"No, it didn't suit me very well. I was a romantic, and had no interest in such matters. Of course, I could not tell the Nazis war didn't suit me. All the young men—boys, really—were fed to the front like cattle. It was the Fuehrer's will."

"One thing I can say about being a soldier, Michael, is that I did a lot of walking. I learned a lot about the men I fought with on the endless, muddy march to Moscow, and if I learned anything it was that human nature is unfathomable."

"Marco came from Oldenburg, a city by the Nordsee. The region by the sea is called Ostfriesland, and the people there are traditionally very tall, sometimes up to seven feet."

"Really? Seven feet? That's a giant!" exclaimed Michael.

"Well, not quite, but close. Marco was actually short, and I could not help but make jokes about his stature. He was good-natured and cheerful, and joked back with me saying that the most popular church in Munich was the Hofbrauhaus. He may have been right!" Friedreich's laughter filled the cozy room.

Michael looked at his mother. "One day, when you are older," she said smiling.

"Marco and I felt like brothers separated at birth. Perhaps it was the fear that united us. We talked of everything young men talk about—women, cars, music, beer—everything. Sometimes late at night when the artillery boomed in the distance, we talked about what it felt like to clutch the damp earth and wait to die."

Friedreich's eyes got distant again. Michael wished he could walk with him through the past, hear the guns roar and the planes rumble overhead. Friedreich tapped the spent tobacco out of his pipe and continued.

"Tobias always hovered about like a vulture. He felt my dislike for him, and it made him suspicious. Often he tried to steal my journal. Tobias, the perfect Nazi, had no mind of his own. He took everything from Hitler—his politics, his strategies, even his hatred for the Jews. Such a man is worse than Hitler, Michael, for it is men like Tobias that make a Hitler possible.

"Tobias shot me as I stole away. He could not tolerate the individual outside of the group. I do not think he gave the individual any worth.

"I deserted the night after Marco's death. In war, little ceremony is given to the dead. I almost missed Marco's burial altogether.

"Hanno, the fisherman from Lindau, woke me early. It struck me that morning how old and tired he looked. With his face wrapped in dirty rags, he could not talk but his eyes spoke of a great sadness. He beckoned me to follow him.

"I quickly dressed and followed him out into the cold. I had no idea of what to expect. The men were unusually quiet, and they looked away from me as if guilty with some secret knowledge. I followed Hanno's silent, hulking frame as we crunched through the hard snow.

"Near a small clearing, he turned toward me and pulled the rags from his mouth. His face, rough with stubble, matched his foul breath.

"'Es tut mir lied,' he whispered, his weathered hand clutching my shoulder firmly. I began to protest. Hanno had nothing to be sorry for. Hanno put a finger to his cracked lips and pointed ahead.

"Several prisoners were filling a grave in the middle of the clearing. Tobias stood behind them, casually holding his gun at his waist. His eyes became sharp with cunning and ill-disguised humor as he noticed me.

"'Halt!' he commanded, and the gaunt men stopped digging. Tobias motioned me over.

"There, half-covered with dirt, lay Marco. His face was deathly pale like an angel's. At that moment something inside me gave, like the rickety support of an old bridge, and a demon rose in my throat.

"'He died for the fatherland. The untermensch shall pay two-fold for his sacrifice!' hissed Tobias, turning his weapon on the trembling diggers.

"All the savagery, all the pain, all the horror of the invasion merged into that single moment. I howled, and the demon spilled forth.

"I snatched a shovel from the nearest digger and beat him severely. He tried to cover his face and fell to his knees, and still I beat him. He collapsed on to the snow, his body half in the fresh grave, and I continued to beat him.

"The other prisoner began to run towards the trees. Tobias shot him in the back and then again on the ground. The reports of the shots echoed through the forest.

"I dropped the shovel. Sweat covered me and I fell, rocking myself back and forth on the cold, hard ground as the madness seeped out of me.

"Tobias walked over and tried to pull me up. 'Marco is dead. Get up!'

"I held my head with my hands and would not rise. I did not want to see the man I had beaten to death."

Inside, Michael began to change. His father, the center of his existence, was no longer among the heavenly host but tinged with darkness. He shuddered.

"I spent the rest of the day in my tent. Nobody bothered me. I organized my gear and waited for night to fall.

"It was particularly cold that evening, and the wind swooped through the iced tree limbs making spectral music. The moon was a mere sliver in the sky, and only the brightest stars shone overhead.

"I followed the path down to Marco's grave. A small cross had been erected in front of it.

"Suddenly a figure stepped out from the cover of the trees. It was the night watch. The soldier's face was protected from the elements, but I knew the figure in an instant—it was Tobias.

"I advanced towards Marco's grave, the weight of my pistol tucked in the small of my back reassuring me as I advanced.

"'What are you doing up so late, Friedreich?' Tobias asked.

"'I came to see Marco.'

"'Marco is *dead*.' Tobias stated it coldly and with much emphasis.

"I nodded and began to turn back to the camp. Two steps down the path I drew my gun and opened fire. Tobias' body shuddered with the damage. He squeezed off a wild burst which walked up the path and hit me in the leg. Then he collapsed, his face arrogant and assuming even in death.

"Behind me, the camp began to stir. I quickly removed my helmet and placed it on the cross. The demon which had been born in the clearing that day was now placed to final rest, and I disappeared into the night, shutting out the fiery pain in my leg and concentrating on the uncertain path ahead."

"Then you met mother," stated Michael.

"Yes. I raced all through the night, getting ever closer to the Russian front. I managed to construct a crude lean-to and start fires for warmth, but I had lost a lot of blood and needed medical attention if I was to live. I ran out of food quickly and was unable to hunt. Your mother was part of a small partisan patrol which discovered my camp. She saved my life, and blessed me with a new one, one worth living."

Friedreich looked over at Natasha, and together they traveled back and lived the day over again.

"And the others?" asked Michael, as fascinated with the noble Marco and the villainous Tobias as he was with King Arthur's knights.

"Other what? Women?" asked Friedreich bemused.

"No, other Nazis!" Michael cried in exasperation.

"Well, there was Claus, the arrogant marksman. I think Claus always thought of the war as a hunting trip. Hunting for people, that is. Funny man, Claus. He had a way of talking about himself as if he wasn't there."

"What do you mean?" asked Michael.

"Well, he would say things like, 'That Claus is quite a shot,' or 'If Claus were in Berlin, things would be different'."

"That Michael is very smart," chimed the boy.

"He learns quickly, eh?" asked Natasha, cocking an eyebrow.

"Too quickly," muttered Friedreich. "I have already told you about Hanno, the fisherman from Lindau and his stories of the green merpeople and their castles beneath the sea."

"Tell me again!" insisted Michael.

"There are not enough hours in the day!" replied Friedreich in exasperation. He stood up to retrieve his bag of tobacco from the windowsill and watched as the sun lowered and then gilded the treetops.

Natasha walked over and wrapped her arms around Friedreich, enjoying the stillness of the moment.

Michael had seen them stand by the window in this manner many times, but he would never see them again in the same light. His imagination wrapped them in various guises. His mother strolling the banks of the Dnieper with a new summer hat. His father towering over the fallen paratrooper waiting to shoot.

The fire in the oven had burned down to embers. Michael shivered, got up, and joined the new strangers in their warmth.

ABOUT THE AUTHOR

R. David Fulcher is a twenty-nine year old author of poetry, science fiction, fantasy and horror fiction. His work has appeared in numerous small press publications, including Heliocentric Net, Gateways, Shadowfeast, The Reaper, Frightnet, Silken Ropes, Twilight Showcase, The Martian Wave, Burning Sky, The Fiction Network, Shadowlands, Lovecraft's Mystery Magazine, Weird Times, Just Write, Writer's Open Forum, The Barrelhouse, Tales from the Grave Audiozine, and Vampires Anonymous. In addition, he is the editor of the small press magazine Samsara.

R. David Fulcher resides in Ashburn, Virginia.

www.ingramcontent.com/pod-product-compliance
Ingram Content Group UK Ltd.
Pitfield, Milton Keynes, MK11 3LW, UK
UKHW040017200726
13854UKWH00001B/242

9 780759 623590